THE GREAT APPALACHIAN REDEMPTION

Alec Neu

For Jake Guthrie and Gladys Neu,

and for West Virginia, my home.

CONTENTS

PREFACE
THE GREAT APPALACHIAN DILEMMA

There's this saying – the heart wants what it wants – which means that our minds, though they try to interfere, have just about no say in the matters of the heart. We just like what we like. We cannot think our way into liking things. We just, simply, like them. And there ain't nothin' we can do about it, neither. That thing we like may not be too pretty, or bright, or sought after by many – it may even be judged or mocked, but all that stuff doesn't matter because it's *ours*, and that's special enough.

There's this other saying – home is where the heart is – which, if our first saying is true, and I reckon it oughtta be, means that we can't logic or reason our way into finding a home, either. Our minds don't pick the place we call home...our heart does. Some hearts find homes in certain lands or cities, while others find their homes amongst specific people or animals.

As our hearts go around, attaching themselves to whatever they please, we have newfound opportunity to find joy, meaning, and comfort in our lives, but it comes at a price, and that price is the possibility for hurt. For different people, this hurt can show up in the loss of a loved one, in the loss of a pet, or, for others, in the loss of a home. This means that no matter what, if our hearts have tied themselves to something, we are always at risk of losing that thing, and that's where the hurt can find us.

For us hill people, those born and raised in West Virginia and the Appalachian mountains, our hearts have tied themselves so uniquely to this land *and* its people, which gives us the chance for significant meaning *and* significant hurt. On one hand, you'll just about never find a friendlier place nor a more gorgeous landscape, but on the other hand, you'll also never find a place so full of unwarranted elitism, social isolation, and the destruction of that same gorgeous landscape which is the defining trait of the region. Whether or not you see the first or the second side of this coin sometimes depends on your location within the state, other times in the circles you hang around, and then there are times when seeing the good or bad side of West Virginia's coin feels about as up to chance as if you had flipped that exact coin and left it up to a game of heads or tails.

This dichotomy leads to a tear in our hearts – on one end, a pull to revel in the comfort within our homes and the love for our state, and on the other, a pull to go out and find a place that isn't so critical and lonely, one with more opportunity and life. This leads many young folks to have conflicting feelings about whether or not to 'stick around' once they're out of school. Many love being with their families but hate the lack of social activity and modernity, while others may enjoy the land and the simplicity of the towns but wish to get away from toxic home lives or friend groups.

All of this culminates into a significant pressure on the coming-of-age West Virginian to throw the baby out with the bathwater, per se - to leave the state and pursue greener grasses elsewhere - disregarding any attachment their hearts hold to the state altogether. And yet, almost inevitably, when they do leave, a part of their heart doesn't go with them. It stays here, in West Virginia, where it will continue to call them home. And many of these people, after years of being gone, do answer this call, choosing to travel down these country roads in order to make their hearts whole again. Others choose to not answer this call at all, favoring peace of mind over peace of heart, and they shouldn't be blamed for their decision, either. There ain't no right or wrong here, just the great Appalachian dilemma, and it is up to each person to choose for themselves what their path will be.

CHAPTER ONE

ORWELL, WEST VIRGINIA

There is a folktale in these parts about leaving home, though I would hardly call it a fiction, for it's as real as the dirt we walk on, and maybe more so. It took place, or...well...it maybe still takes place. It's hard to say, really, but suffice to say that this folktale is about the people of Appalachia and will always be that way. It's a story as old as these mountains, and yet it has never been told until now.

This story begins in the small town of Orwell, West Virginia. For anyone from the region, they've surely visited an Orwell or two in their time. It's a small manufacturing town that has seen its day, made up of old factory warehouses, dirty brick shops, and small single-family homes with metal awnings. Orwell is a quiet town. All the factories are closed, of course, and their former workers are well into retirement. Back in the day, Main Street would have been bustling with business, events, and people engaging in communal activities, but these days, the streets are quiet, and the only church in town just lost two of its remaining eight members. Next Sunday, the pastor is going to propose shutting down from lack of funds, even though some of its members have been going to that church since it was built half a century ago. That's just the way it is.

Most people leave town if they can – unless they have to tend to their parents or something like that. Nobody blames them either. These folks go off in search of better jobs or a more exciting life. They'll probably find it, too. They'll joke when they leave about how nothing goes on back at home, but we make do with what we have. It's easy to jab at the poverty and loneliness that are married to this area, but those who have stuck around know how far we've come. The past generations worked tooth and nail to give their families a better life. Immigrants fleeing war and poverty came here for a new chance. They worked the mines and the factories and made their living any way they could. And now that those workers are old and broken, they sit on their porch or in their living rooms as their children go off to find something better. Such is the nature of generations, but it hasn't done any favors for Orwell.

Of the families that have stayed behind, their children have no shortage of outdoor space to roam. West Virginia is known for its scenery, after all. They go hunting, fishing, hiking, swimming, and the like. It's better than sitting at home bored all day. For some, it beats being around the unhealthy living conditions associated with such an area. They're just happy to get away from their quiet town, biding their time until one day they, too, can leave and never look back.

Our tale starts as two such kids are walking home from school on the railroad tracks, as many kids in this area do. Many outsiders would call this way to get home dangerous, but the locals know that the rail system isn't what it used to be, so you really don't see that many trains come through – maybe one per day. The only consistent train is the one that goes to Huxley – that fancy town out east, just beyond the border of the state. Everybody has seen Huxley's advertisements on the television and the radio. It's a city of complete luxury – jampacked with restaurants, events, nightlife, and every form of entertainment you could imagine.

Huxley isn't that far away from Orwell, maybe a two-hour drive...but you can't access it by car because no roads travel to it. The only way to get to the Great City is by purchasing one of their enormously expensive train tickets, an amount of which even a person of above-average income would have to save up awhile for. All the kids beg their parents for tickets to vacation or to move there, but with jobs paying so little in the area, it's hard enough to feed everyone in the family and keep a roof over their heads, let alone take a trip to a luxurious city. Here's one thing we all know, though – once someone can afford a ticket to a place like Huxley, they don't come back. In fact, nobody here has seen a person take that train out of town and ever return. Maybe the grass is greener there. It probably is.

Walking on the railroad tracks this fall day are Noah and Ali, two eighth graders who have been friends since they were babies. Though they are the subjects of our story, it is important to know they are no different than any other kids. Average students, mostly. Ali has a slight edge over Noah academically, but he can't be blamed for his poor grades on account of his home life. It's sad, but not uncommon around here. They are planning to do what they do every day – walk home on the tracks and find some way to entertain themselves until school starts in the morning.

"I miss Jake." Ali said. "Do you think he's okay?"

"I don't know." Noah looked down. "The longer he's gone the more I'm imagining that somethin' bad happened to him."

"I don't wanna believe it." Ali insisted. "But I don't know what alternative there is. He's a good kid. I'm just scared."

"It's been four days." Noah said. "Some people have been out lookin' for him, but I doubt they'll keep it up for long."

"I don't like thinkin' about it." Ali looked off into the tree line. "But all I know is that he better not have gone on some stupid make-believe quest again and not told us about it. I'll whoop him if I find out that's what has happened. He's about scared me half to death."

After a couple minutes of walking, the two friends felt a rumbling on the tracks.

"Huxley train." Noah called out. The two kids stepped out of the way and waited for it to pass. After it cleared, they began walking again.

"No chance he took the train outta town, right?" Ali wondered.

"Nah. He couldn't even dream about affording a ticket to Huxley, much less anything else once he got there. It's not in his nature to want that, anyway. That place is too rich for his blood."

"That's true." Ali agreed, drifting off into thought about where her friend had gone off to, and if he was okay.

"Are we playin' games tonight?" Noah asked. He was doing his best to get off the subject.

"Yeah, that sounds good to me."

They walked in silence the rest of the way home, save for saying goodbye as they split off.

Noah got home first. He tried to be quiet as he walked into the house. His dad was asleep on the couch, and it was a bad idea to wake that drunk up under any circumstance. It was best to just stay out of his way. Noah's mom off and married a different guy when he was ten. He goes and visits them every other weekend. The stepdad likes him, but not enough to have him around all the time. Noah knows that his mom has a new life now, and that he just gets to be a visitor.

Ali got home a few minutes later. Both of her parents were still at work at the hospital. The house was nice, clean, and cozy, but she wished her parents worked less and stayed home more. As she walked inside the house, her pit bull Roxy came up to greet her. Roxy was a cute black and white dog – muscular, but not that big. The happy pup's tail pivoted back and forth strongly as Ali gave her a big hug.

"C'mon, girl, let's go upstairs." She said, standing back up, as they both made their way to her bedroom.

After some time chipping away at her homework, Ali messaged Noah and asked if he was ready to get online. He responded almost instantly, saying he was good to go. Ali, Noah, and Jake had been playing the same video game for the past three years, and they were quite good at it. The trio had unparalleled teamwork, but as the two kids played tonight without their friend, it was clear that their rhythm was off. They lost every round they played, and it seemed like no matter what they tried, they couldn't improve.

"What happened to us?" Ali asked Noah. "We're normally killing it."

"It's because of these randoms that keep getting matched on our team." Noah complained, frustrated at their consistent losses. "We need three to have a full squad, and Jake's up and disappeared on us."

"We might need a new game that only does duos…"

"Yeah, maybe. Things are just more fun when Jake's around, though."

They kept playing for another hour with little change in success. During one of the matches, Noah kept noticing a weird sound coming from Ali's headset.

"What's that whining coming from your mic?" Noah asked.

"Whining?" She turned to look at Roxy, who was no longer asleep, and was now looking back and forth between her and the window.

"What is it girl?" Ali asked her. "Need to go outside?"

Roxy was acting weird. Normally she'd walk to the door if she needed to go potty, but this time she walked over and moved the curtains with her nose so she could see out the window.

Ali got up and walked over to clear the curtains out of Roxy's way, and as she drew them open, she looked at Roxy, whose eyes were now wide and fixed, staring off into the wooded area next to her house.

"What do you see?" She asked in that enthusiastic tone people use on their pets. She peered off into the distance, waiting to see the same doe that always walked through the yard with her fawns. But as Ali's eyes focused on the dark yard, she saw an outline of a person standing at the edge of the woods.

"Oh my god!" She yelled as she ducked under the window. "Noah, Noah, Noah. Someone's staring at me."

"What?" Noah questioned. She could hear his voice faintly through the headset.

"Someone is at my house. They're staring at me from the forest." Her breathing became heavy. "I'm scared. Mom and dad aren't home yet."

"Okay, okay." Noah tried to think about what the best next step was. "Wait right there. I'm heading over." He grabbed his house keys, a flashlight, and a pocketknife, and hurried quietly out the door to not disturb his sleeping dad.

It was about a four-minute jog to Ali's house. As he approached the front yard, he slowed down and looked around cautiously, but he didn't see anything of note. He tiptoed his way to the right side of the house, where he saw Ali standing outside, holding her hands up to her head, clearly stressed and panicking.

"What happened?" Noah asked as he approached her, glancing back and forth between her and the forest, wondering if they were in danger.

"It was Jake!" Ali pointed toward the woods. "He started calling my name when I was in my room. I saw him only for a second, but by the time I got outside, he had run off into the forest."

"Come on, Ali..." Noah said doubtingly, worrying that they were both still unsafe. "Are you sure? We should get back inside."

"No, we can't! Noah, we have to go get him. What if he's in trouble?"

Noah paused for a moment, remembering his knife. That at least gave him a little sense of security.

"Um, okay, we can go look for him," Noah told her, "but at the first sign of trouble, you have to leave, lock yourself in the house, and call the cops. Okay? Here's my flashlight."

They both started walking into the woods, standing very close to one another.

"Jake! Jake!" They yelled repeatedly. Ali was lost in the moment, but Noah couldn't help feeling eerie about the situation. He kept looking behind them. Something wasn't right, but they didn't stop.

"This way! Come on, you slackers!" They heard in the distance. Noah recognized Jake's voice. The tone was so frivolous, but the shadowy setting turned it creepy.

"This isn't a joke!" Ali yelled. "Can you just come here?"

Jake's dark figure kept disappearing behind trees, but Ali and Noah did their best to keep up with him.

Eventually, they made their way through the tree line and entered an open field. In the middle of the clearing was one of the town's abandoned factories. It was an ominous, massive silhouette in the moonlight.

"In here!" Jake directed them from a distance. As he said that, Ali whipped the flashlight toward the factory and saw Jake wave his arm at them and then turn around to enter the building. There was no doubt it was him, now. They both got a good glimpse and instantly recognized his short stature, that thick red curly hair, and Jake's signature clothing style – baggy clothes with boots, like he was preparing for his growth spurt to hit at any moment.

"What in the absolute world is he up to?" Noah asked Ali.

"Jake! Are you okay?" Ali shouted toward the building, with no answer.

"I don't like this." Noah took a step back. "I think we need to call the cops."

"It's just Jake." Ali tried to reason with him. "Come on."

They walked through the field and eventually arrived at the same door Jake went in. Ali walked through the door first with little hesitation. Noah followed closely behind.

As they turned the corner, they saw the main floor of the empty factory, only lit by the moonlight coming through the tall, shattered windows. Jake stood in the middle of the factory floor.

"Guys!" Jake exclaimed, raising his arms up. "You made it!"

Ali turned off the flashlight, dropped it, ran up, and hugged him.

"Oh my god I thought you were dead." She said.

"I'm okay." He assured her.

Noah approached hesitantly as Jake turned his attention to him.

"Hey, man, you okay?" Noah asked, as he reached for a paranoid side hug.

"Yeah, I'm okay. Don't worry guys." Jake tried to calm their nerves.

"What happened to you?" Ali wondered. "We've been so worried."

"I've been in here." Jake looked around the space and held his hands out to both sides.

"But...why?" Ali asked her friend. "The whole town's been looking for you."

"I want to tell you why I've been gone, but you have to promise you won't freak out." Jake requested.

Ali knew he was up to another scheme.

"Honestly, man, I'm already kind of freaking out." Noah replied.

"Look, dude." Jake said, once again inviting Noah to look around the room. "Everything is okay."

"Okay, well then tell us quickly and let's get out of here." Noah demanded.

"You worry too much!" Jake waved his hand toward Noah in a dismissive way. "But if you insist..."

Jake looked up and signaled toward the ceiling, gesturing toward himself this time. Ali and Noah looked at him, confused, until they heard shuffling in the beams above. A second later, a large creature fell and landed just behind Jake, shaking the floor upon impact. It was a dark thing. Tall, maybe six feet. Its back was to them, but it had these huge black wings. Ali and Noah stood still, petrified by the beast's presence.

As it slowly moved its deformed legs to turn itself around, its large, piercing red eyes were revealed. It was like staring into death itself.

Ali gasped. Noah lost his breath. Both of their hearts were ready to collapse.

"It's okay, it's okay." Jake attempted to mitigate panic, holding his hands out to them. "He's friendly."

"Friendly?!" Ali yelled as she backpedaled away from it. "What do you mean it's..." She paused, locking eyes with the beast. Her backpedaling stopped. "Wait, Jake, is that the..."

"Yes, it is." Jake confirmed.

Ali and Noah stood frozen, simultaneously in horror and wonder as they stared at the hideous, deformed monster in front of them.

"I...I..." Ali struggled to find words. "I...This can't be real. The Mothman isn't real."

"Well, of course he is!" Jake defended, pointing his arms at the obvious moth person in front of them. "I found him! And he needs our help."

"Uhhhhhh, no." Noah denied the motion, shaking his head and backing up a bit, still staring into the monster's piercing red eyes. "We don't want to help him, Jake."

"You just don't know him!" Jake defended.

"I think I know enough!" Noah rebutted. "From the stories. He brings death and tragedy to anyone who sees him. Years ago, he destroyed that bridge and killed all those people. I think I know enough to say we should get out of here, like now."

"I did not destroy the bridge." A voice spoke to the kids, but the sound didn't emanate from the creature. The voice was inside their heads.

Noah and Ali, stunned by the telepathic message, shot their hands up to their skulls, applied pressure, and winced as if they were in pain. Jake stood there, casually watching them.

"What was that?!" Noah panickily asked, looking around.

"I'm in front of you." The voice pointed out.

"You're not moving your mouth." Noah returned.

"I do not have the ability to speak." The creature volleyed. "This is how I communicate."

"Really cool, right guys?" Jake said, nonchalantly. He turned to Ali. "Hey, how's Roxy?"

"Jake." Ali shot a firm glare at him. "Roxy is at home. Can we talk about the telepathic monster for a sec?"

"Yeah, I was getting there! Geez." Jake backed off. "You guys are freaking out way too much over this. He's not dangerous."

It was hard for Ali and Noah to believe their friend while they were staring into the Mothman's predatory red eyes. They didn't know what to do, so they just stood there in silence.

"Come on, y'all." Jake tried to reason with them. "If he wanted to hurt us, he would've done so already, right? Let's move on."

"Okay, that's true, I guess." Ali cautiously understood, feeling a little tension leave the room.

"Why did you want us to meet this thing, Jake?" Noah interrogated.

"Perhaps I can help explain why you're here." The voice answered, sending another telepathic message into Noah and Ali's minds.

"Jesus Christ!" Noah shouted, holding his head once more. "Can you please, like, speak quietly or something? I feel like my head is going to explode."

"I can try." The voice answered. "Now, I want to ask both of you...do you enjoy being here, in this town?"

The kids stood there for a moment, confused.

"I don't know what that has to do with...." Ali started.

"No, I don't like it here." Noah interrupted. Ali looked at him, concerned.

"What? I don't." Noah defended. "I hate living here. My dad's a jerk, our town sucks, and my mom doesn't even want me around. I love you guys, but you're about all I have." He turned back to the Mothman. "So what's the deal? Are you gonna be our savior and fly the three of us somewhere better?"

Jake mumbled something under his breath.

"What was that, Jake?" Noah addressed his friend.

"I was just sayin'..." Jake looking down and shrugged his shoulders a bit, "if you already know *so* much about the Mothman, then you should know that he can't carry people anywhere."

"Oh...right." Noah remembered. "Well, I forgot." He turned his attention back to the monster. "Then what do you want from us?" He winced in preparation for another loud response.

"All I want to offer you is a better life." The voice spoke, more softly this time. "This place was not always as bad as it is now. In fact, there was a time when this land was so beautiful, it was once confused with heaven itself. And even as it fell away from that, the people used to be nicer and more compassionate...everyone helped each other."

"Sure, my grandma used to tell me about times like that." Ali stepped in. "But I don't think anything any of us can do is just going to change that overnight."

"You're not wrong." The voice replied. "But all things worth doing take hard work and time. We could build it back."

"Quite frankly," Noah paused, looking off toward the shattered windows, thinking about what he wanted to say, "I don't want to make this place better. I would rather just go somewhere else that actually *is* better and let this place crumble to the ground."

"I understand." The Mothman told him. "Which is why I am presenting to you an opportunity to get out of this state and see all there is for you beyond these borders. All I ask in return is that you help me with one task."

"Well, I'm not surprised there's a catch." Noah said cynically. "But I'm willing to bite if it means getting out of here. What's the task?"

"I need to mend the wounds I have inflicted on this land." The voice answered.

"You mean how you've terrorized people for decades and made them afraid to live here?" Noah asked.

"No, for something much deeper than that." The voice replied, rather cryptically.

"I'm not sure I see what you're getting at." Noah looked at the monster, waiting for him to explain.

"In order for you to understand the task at hand," the creature told them, "you need to, first, understand my history. It goes farther back than you know. In fact, it goes farther back than anyone knows. And only after you know the truth about how I got here – how we all got here – will you be able to make a clear decision on whether or not to help."

"Okay, let's hear it then." Noah encouraged.

"Jake?" The Mothman queued.

Jake walked away from the monster and joined his friends.

"Come on guys, sit down." Jake said. "He's going to show us."

Ali and Noah shared a questioning glance with each other, trying to see what Jake meant by that.

"Hear him out." Jake requested.

The Mothman dropped into a sitting position, the dust kicking up to his sides.

"Sit...sit!" Jake insisted, waving his hands toward the ground.

Ali slowly sat down first, with suspicion. Noah followed.

"Jake, please explain to them how this works." The voice requested.

"Noah." Jake turned to his friend. "You know anything about Mothman's prophecies?"

"A little bit." Noah answered. "It's like the visions he gives to people in their dreams...or something like that."

"Yes, exactly." Jake confirmed. "That's how he's going to show us where he came from. He's going to give us a vision."

As he said that, the Mothman's eyes turned bright yellow. It was clear he was no longer mentally present in the room.

"Look." Jake pointed to the creature, asking his friends to focus on him.

Ali curiously gazed over in the monster's direction and then suddenly became still, sitting on the floor, her eyes now yellow like the Mothman's.

"Ali.....Ali...." Noah grabbed her arm and shook her a bit, but it was clear to him that she was absent-minded as well. It scared him a bit, feeling like he might lose control of himself if he looked at the creature.

"Come on." Jake told Noah.

Realizing he was too deep into the situation to back out, Noah let out a sigh and looked into the creature's eyes. As he did, his vision flashed into complete whiteness.

"For you to understand what needs to be done to save this land," the voice said, "I need to take you to the beginning of it all – to when it was born."

CHAPTER TWO

APPALACHIAN ORIGINS

The Mothman revealed a dream-like vision to the kids and began to explain all that they were seeing.

This land should look familiar to you. It is your home, although long before the humans arrived. Look at the abundance of trees, the clear skies, and the fall colors. Here, there was peace. Here, we had contentment. Look at all the animal life all around. See everything working in harmony.

I can feel you wondering where it all came from. Well, I can assure you it wasn't from me, nor my ancestors. It's hard to know exactly how it all happened. The higher we reach for understanding, the more abstract it all becomes. All I know is that when Gods of the Old World came across this place, they called it Hesper. They knew it was as close to paradise as one could get on Earth, and so they decided to create a new system here – one that would not repeat the mistakes that had plagued their old lands.

Knowing humans would one day inhabit these hills, the Gods of Old created an order which consisted of two Keepers, named Selu and Kanati. It is important to note that these beings were just as powerful as the Gods of Old, yet nowhere close to having any supreme power over the world. Instead, it was their mission to keep this land and its people safe – to establish and maintain harmony within nature and to provide humans with the best lives they could have.

The first of these two Keepers was Selu – the goddess of flora – and she was beautiful in every way. She possessed a loving spirit that gave unconditionally to her humans. Every day, she would go outside and dance through the fields. She would twirl up the mountain and skip back down to the valley. Every place her feet touched, the most beautiful flowers and trees would spring up from the ground. From this dance, she produced an abundance of fruits and vegetables for the humans – all which would grow spontaneously from the earth. With Selu's gifts, the humans never wanted for food, and she never wanted anything from them in return.

The other Keeper was Selu's partner Kanati – the god of fauna. It was his job to watch over the animals of this land and to provide their protection. The wildlife was deeply grateful for the security that Kanati provided them, and their connection eventually grew so deep that Kanati could even converse with them. He understood the animals, and they understood him. Out of gratitude for his gift of longevity, when the animal knew it was time for its life to come to an end, it would come to Kanati and offer its life to him. He would then take the animal and use its hide and meat to keep the humans warm and fed. And in this way, all life had balance and cycled into each other.

Seeing the humans happy made Selu and Kanati happy, and they did every-thing they could to make sure the humans wanted for nothing. This made the New Lands abundant with life, and joy, and peace. The people of this land spent their time creating beautiful works of art, holding festivals, and exploring the wondrous nature this place had to offer.

But, after eras and eras of prosperity, the humans multiplied to a point that became burdensome on the great Keepers. New tribes began to populate regions that had never been inhabited by humans. Selu's dance could no longer cover such vast distances, nor could Kanati provide protection for so many animals. The humans became at risk of starving, so the two Keepers began to think about what should be done.

After great contemplation, Kanati and Selu decided to have children so there could be additional gods who could aid with the workload. When these children finally arrived into this world, Selu and Kanati were overjoyed. They had given birth to one daughter – Nimkii – and one son – Ani.

Ani was a majestic thunderbird, which meant that he could soar through the skies at great speeds, covering the distances that would be impossible for his parents. He possessed a wingspan of almost twenty feet, and when his wings flapped in the sky, the wind would rumble in all directions.

Nimkii, on the other hand, was a brilliant goddess in human form who possessed the power of electricity. She would use her mind to create the most amazing devices, which she would then power using her electricity. These devices drastically increased the efficiency of the workload on Selu and Kanati and improved the homes and livelihoods of the humans she looked after.

Eventually, Nimkii found a way to repel her electricity against the earth's magnetic field, which gave her the power to levitate. After that, she and her brother would play in the skies for hours, and the humans would watch them from below in amazement. The flashes of electricity from Nimkii and the loud, thunderous claps of Ani's wings would strike awe in the humans who witnessed them, realizing the sheer strength of their power.

Selu and Kanati were grateful beyond measure for their children, and the humans were, too. The threats of low food resources and intertribal conflict had subsided for the moment, but they had not been entirely eradicated. One day, Nimkii had an idea about how to get rid of this problem forever, so she went to her mother talk about her ideas.

· • · • · • · • · ·

"Mom..." She began. "I want to teach the humans how I make electricity."

"Why on Earth do you want to do that?" Selu wondered.

"Well, there are just so many tribes now." Nimkii explained. "And it gets worse every day. I've noticed that they are beginning to lose their sense of community. It is sad to see, but they are being driven into isolation by war, greed, and their fear of outsiders. But Mom, I know my devices can bring them together again, improve their communication, and even end their suffering. I've had dreams of the future after giving them my powers – where the humans have made the most amazing things – like vessels that let them travel quickly between tribes. Can you imagine that, Mom? If they had more power, I really do think the humans would be able to find what is best for them. They might not even need us anymore after a while! They could find their own peace and unity, in whatever way works for them."

"But honey, the humans often do not know what is best for them." Selu told her daughter. "That is why we cannot give them such a power. They may hurt themselves. Remember, there is an order to things. It is our job to provide for them. They have their own tasks to deal with."

"I just want to help them."

"I know. But do you remember what your father said?"

"He said that if we ever revealed the secret of our powers to the humans, that he would take our powers away forever." Nimkii answered.

"That's right. And you don't want to lose your powers, do you?"

"No, Mom."

· · · · ● · ● · · · ·

Nimkii was unhappy with this verdict. Even though she was told she wasn't allowed to pursue her dreams, thoughts about giving the humans her powers kept entering her mind. Nimkii would spend her nights romanticizing about huge cities with the tallest buildings she could imagine, ones that would touch the clouds as she does. She imagined the humans would eventually make devices that would keep them from dying, so no person would ever experience loss again. These thoughts weighed on her heavily, until one day she went to her brother Ani for help.

· · · · ● · ● · · · ·

"Ani, I want to show the humans how I create electricity." Nimkii told him. *"And you can show them how to fly, too, if you want. I want the humans to live as we do."*

"Are you crazy?" Ani inquired. *"Dad will kill us."*

"No, he won't. We can distract him...and mom. Not for long...just for enough time until they see all that the humans can be. I know if we had a chance to show them that their rule is stupid, they would eventually understand."

"Nimkii, I don't like where your head is at. Mom and Dad have never led us down the wrong path."

"They haven't," Nimkii agreed, "but they're old. They're stuck in their ways. The humans are evolving. Things are different now. Don't you see? Why don't you want to help me?"

"I do want to help you, but I'm afraid of what will happen. Just think about all that could go wrong if I taught the humans how to fly. What if they left us for good? What if they flew away and never came back?"

"Then don't teach them to fly." Nimkii replied. "Let me teach them electricity, and that way, if I get in trouble, I'll take all the blame. I'll lose my powers, but you'll keep yours. Deal?"

"There's no talking you out of this, is there?"

"I don't think I can live with myself if I don't give it a shot."

Ani sighed. "Okay, you've got a deal. What do you need me to do?"

· · · · ● · ● · · ·

Nimkii revealed her plan to Ani – they would each take one parent and find a way to restrict them for enough time until Nimkii could teach the humans how to make electricity.

The two kids split up and began working on their traps, which they planned to spring at dawn.

That night, Nimkii built a device that, once triggered, would temporarily trap her father in a metal box. There was no way to get out from the inside, so she would have more than enough time to carry out the rest of her plan.

Ani, not having the craftiness of his sister, decided to dig a deep, deep hole in the ground on the path where Selu would dance every day. He covered it with twigs and leaves, hoping she wouldn't notice.

The next morning, the kids stayed close to their traps, but still out of sight, waiting to see if their plan would be successful.

Selu was the first to leave the house. As she walked into the field and began her dance, corn and potatoes and beautiful wildflowers sprung up all around her. Ani watched from a distance, filled with worry. His mother danced and danced with such merriment that she didn't even come close to noticing the trap her son had set for her. She began to skip as she drew closer to it, and she even skipped such a great distance that she nearly cleared the hole in its entirely, but as her back foot came down, it found no ground. Selu's eyes opened wide in panic as she struggled to find her balance. Her front foot slipped out from under her as she fell backwards, plummeting into the hole. Ani felt a brief moment of joy from the success of his trap, until a few seconds later, when a snap rang from the pit and his mother cried out in pain.

"Help!" She yelled. "Somebody, help me! Please, I think my legs are broken. Somebody, please! Help me!"

Ani flew over to the hole, terrified. He never thought his trap was going to hurt her.

"Mom!" Ani yelled as he approached and looked into the dark pit, unable to see her.

"Ani, please, help me out of here!" His mother cried. "I'm in so much pain."

Regret fell over him, but he wasn't sure what to do. If he pulled her out now, the whole plan would have been for nothing.

"Mom, I'm so sorry." Ani fought through his regret. "I'm going to go get Nimkii. We'll be back to help you in no time."

He flew off across the field and into the trees to find his sister, hearing his mother's cries fade behind him. He realized this was a terrible idea and had to find a way to right his wrongs as soon as he could.

· · · · · ◆ · ◆ · · ·

At the same time, Nimkii was waiting for her own trap to spring. She watched from the hillside as her father walked through the woods. Along his walk, he spotted a buck whose antlers she had tangled up in a vine. She knew her father could not resist helping an animal in need. As Kanati approached the helpless animal in an attempt to free it, he stepped directly onto the trigger switch for Nimkii's trap. A click sounded. Instantaneously, metal walls began to shoot upward to contain the god within the metal box his daughter had created.

Kanati panicked, realizing he was being trapped. He jumped to yell for Selu, and as he leapt and yelled, the roof on the box quickly slid shut and separated his head from his body. Nimkii screamed in terror as she watched her father's head roll off of the metal box and fall onto the ground.

She stood there, frozen in shock, and didn't move a muscle until moments later when Ani arrived.

"Nimkii...Nimkii...I need help!" He called out while approaching her. "Mom's in trouble."

As he neared his sibling, he noticed the petrified look on her face.

"What happened? What's wrong with you?" He asked her, turning to look where she was looking. It was then that he witnessed the horror for himself – his father's head, lying on the ground below.

"Nimkii, what have you done?!" He yelled as he ran over to the box, looking for a way to free his father's body in some frantic attempt to save the situation.

"I just wanted to keep him contained!" Nimkii yelled in a strained voice, tears beginning to well up in her eyes. "He got scared and tried to jump out."

The electric god fell to her knees, covered her face with her hands, and began to sob uncontrollably. Ani continued his attempt to dismantle the trap.

"Ani, stop." Nimkii begged.

He kept trying to find a way to free his dad's body.

"Ani...stop!" She yelled. "It's no use. He's dead."

Her words smacked Ani into reality. He backed away from the box, tears filling his eyes, as he looked down at his father's head, which sat on the ground, motionless.

"But..." He stared blankly at it. "He can't be."

Just then, a loud rush of air came from behind them. Ani and Nimkii turned around fast because it startled them. Walking toward them was a woman they did not recognize – one of astounding beauty, strength, and posture. She had a spear in her left hand and a bow on her back. A crescent moon was fixed in her hair. She walked slowly but confidently over to the restrained buck, crouched, and began to untangle its antlers from the vines.

The kids were bewildered by this strange person's appearance. Ani couldn't hold back his curiosity of who would intrude in such a dire moment.

"Excuse me." He said to her. "Can you please back away. This is not a good place to be right now."

"This is the exact place I need to be...right now." The woman said.

Ani and Nimkii, with tears still in their eyes, looked at each other, then back at the woman.

"Who are you?" Nimkii asked. "Why are you here?"

"I am Artemis, goddess of Greece, of the Old Lands." She spoke sternly but didn't bother to look at either of the kids. She stayed close to her task. "I'm here because you two just made a whole mess of things, didn't you?"

"I......um.....We....." Ani stuttered, not sure where to start.

"That question was rhetorical." Artemis annoyedly denied. "You don't need to explain a thing. I already know what has happened here." She looked down at the severed head, then gave a quick visual inspection of the box that Kanati's body was still in, before going back to untangling the vines.

Nimkii wiped the tears from her eyes and stood up.

"Artemis, you have to help us. We can explain everything!"

"Do you not listen, child?!" Artemis outburst at the girl. "From now on, I want silence from you both." She waved her hand toward them. Nimkii tried to argue but found that no words left her mouth.

"There will be no more speaking from either of you." The Greek goddess told them. "That way you cannot cause any more trouble."

Artemis freed the last strand of vine around the buck's antlers and turned back to the siblings.

"Besides," she said as she stood up and cleared her hands of debris, "your punishment has already been rendered. I have been sent here to deliver it to you."

Ani and Nimkii were so scared and confused. They didn't mean to do any harm. What did this woman mean by "punishment"? They didn't even know who she was. All they wanted in that moment was to be alone, so they could figure out what the next best step was for themselves.

"It's a shame..." Artemis let out an unempathetic sigh and shook her head in disapproval, "but this has to be done." She revealed a scroll from her tunic and began to read.

"Ani and Nimkii, you have created an imbalance in the system set up for you by the Gods of Old. As such, you shall be given punishments befitting the crimes you have waged here today."

The goddess turned to Ani.

"Ani the Thunderbird, you have cost your mother the ability to walk and dance, and so your legs shall be forever broken."

As she said that, the Great Bird's legs snapped in half, and he went to cry out in pain, but his scream made no noise. Water filled his eyes.

"You have conspired against the Gods of Old and the Order of That Which is Above, and so are henceforth cast out from our graces. As your father was once loved by all the animals of the earth, now, you will be feared by them."

She snapped her fingers, and Ani's wings began to burn. He fell to the ground as he was deformed and turned into an ugly, menacing creature – half man, half insect. His eyes turned bright red, his wings black, and two large, knife-like teeth grew out of his face.

"Now, any animal that sees you will run in fear. It will know from your eyes that you intend it harm, and so you shall never gain the trust with the animals, or the humans, that your father once had. You will go hungry, and so will the humans who your father fed so generously."

The goddess turned her attention to Nimkii, whose eyes were filled with fear upon seeing the deformation of her brother.

"And for you, the one who thought she was smarter than the great Logic of the world – the one who is the root cause of this horrific mess - you will first and foremost be set eternally ablaze for your terrible misdeeds."

As Artemis spoke those words, Nimkii's body caught fire, and a flame wrapped around her head. Nimkii fell to her knees as the intense heat scorched her body.

"Your brother was merely an accessory in this sinister plot of yours, and as such, you shall be charged as the primary actor regarding the fate of your mother." Artemis looked back down at the scroll.

"Since she will never be able to walk the Earth again, your fate will be the same."

Nimkii's legs began to squeeze until her bones shattered. They shriveled and began to wilt away until they had vanished completely.

"Your mother once danced and brought fertility to the land." Artemis continued. "Now all you shall bring is its destruction."

The flame that consumed Nimkii intensified.

"With this fire," she continued, *"any living thing you touch will be burned, and you shall walk this earth no more, forever floating in the skies, unable to tend to the land as your mother so generously did."*

Nimkii's body began to levitate a foot above the ground as she writhed in agony.

"From this day forth, you shall bear a dress made of hot copper, so that any embrace you wish for will burn your beloved. You will never know love, and the people you so blindly tried to save will now have to toil and work hard, difficult labor for the entirety of their lives to produce the same crops which your mother so easily made for them."

Nimkii's eyes turned black, and her hands deformed from the heat of the flames. A copper dress appeared and wrapped itself around her, hissing from the hot metal's interaction with the humid air around it.

"Thus is the decree of the Council from the Gods of the Old Lands." Artemis said, closing the scroll.

The goddess walked over to the buck and grabbed its antler as she swung herself into a mount. Once she was situated, she looked at the two monsters who were doubled over in immeasurable pain from her punishments. The Greek goddess' face displayed no sign of regret regarding what she had done. Ani and Nimkii had to lay there, helpless, unable to speak or scream or plea for her to undo this terrible curse.

"I am heading north, to the original human camp." Artemis said to them. *"I will teach them to hunt so they have a chance to survive. A fellow goddess will join me to teach them the ways of agriculture. I will not lift the muteness from your tongues, for your words have brought enough damage and offense to all there is. You were once gods. Now all you may be are insectuous beasts, and as*

beasts you shall remain. Do not seek to rectify your misdeeds. They cannot be undone. Do not search for your mother. We have hidden her from your eyes so you cannot cause her any more harm. Now go, far away from this place, and pray I never have to come back to tell you twice."

As she spoke these final words, the goddess tapped the side of the buck with her foot as she held on to the back of its neck, and it sped off with such a pace that she might as well have vanished into thin air.

· · · · ● · ● · · · ·

"And that is how I came to be as I am now," the voice said to the kids as the vision lifted and they all returned to the factory floor. "I am Ani, the Thunderbird, son of the fallen Keepers of these lands, turned a monster by the Gods of Old for the suffering I have brought upon all of you. I wish to redeem that which was lost, to bring us back to the paradise we once had."

"I...I don't know what to say." Noah uttered. "It was all avoidable. All of this misery and pain and hunger and all the absolute *crap* that humans have to deal with. It's all because of one stupid mistake you made?!"

"I am afraid so." The Mothman answered.

"That's so unfair." Ali looked up at the ceiling, trying to make sense of it all. "Maybe I get them punishing you and your sister, but why do all of us have to suffer because of it?"

"I agree." The Mothman said. "And I am sorry things turned out this way. But now you see how we got here. And now you see why I *have* to redeem myself."

"But, if what Artemis said is true," Noah reasoned, "then that means there is no redemption – that we can't get back to the paradise that was in the story. Kanati is dead and Selu is gone. Our fate has been sealed."

"Well, maybe so." Jake interjected. "But we can still make the best of what we have now. You know, try to clean things up! Who knows what could happen if we worked toward it..."

"I don't know." Ali felt defeated knowing that everyone's fate had already been sealed. "It kind of feels like a lost cause to me."

"But you guys don't even know the whole story yet." Jake told his friends. "Ani, tell them about your sister."

"Oh yeah." Ali looked up toward the Mothman. "What happened to her? Is she alive?"

"Yes, Nimkii is still alive." He answered. "But we haven't spoken since the day our parents died. Nimkii couldn't stand staying in the place that caused her heart so much pain. I begged her to stay and help me find a remedy to the disaster we caused, but she made a vow to leave and make a new life for herself elsewhere – to show everyone that her ambition was not in vain."

"Where did she go?" Ali asked.

"She built a new city just outside of the state's border." Ani responded.

"Wait, Huxley is *Nimkii's* creation?!" Noah shot a surprised look over to Jake.

"Yes, it is." Ani answered.

"Oh man, that's awesome." Noah stood in wonder. "I've always wanted to go there!"

"Yeah, me too." Ali agreed. "Which is why I'm having a problem seeing the, um, problem..." She paused. "Is there something wrong with Huxley? Everything I've seen or heard about it makes it sound spectacular."

"I'm sure it is." The Mothman told them. "Nimkii is a goddess of great power and precision. Anything she makes *will* be great. But that is my exact dilemma. Huxley sits outside of West Virginia. Every day, the Great City my sister built attracts more and more people to it. People from our state board that train and never come back. Whether she means to or not, Nimkii is single handedly draining her original home of all its life – a home she was *created to provide life for* – driving it, each day, further and further into poverty and isolation. I'm sure her intentions are pure, but it is my job to bring people back to the state I love, and her ambitious attempt to find her own redemption is in direct conflict with that."

"Shoot." Noah said. "So she just up and abandoned everybody."

"Well, given the circumstances, I can't necessarily blame her." Ali defended.

"I can't either." The Mothman said. "It was her pain that drove her away. Her intentions have always been pure."

"Awh." Ali sympathized with the lightning god's situation. "Well, maybe that pain in her heart will heal one day."

"I hope it does." The Mothman responded. "I would love to have my family back again – or at least what's left of it. And that is exactly where my plan comes in. I think that if we can revitalize this state, Nimkii will be able to overcome the wounds she feels. If we can make this place better, she will finally feel at peace enough to return. But we need people who are actually willing to help us make it better. And, I'm sorry, but three middle schoolers won't be enough."

"I'm guessing that's where we come in." Noah assumed.

"In fact, it is." The Mothman confirmed. "Every day, more and more people board that train to Huxley only to never return. What I want from you three is to go to the Great City and bring as many people back as you can."

Noah let out a little laugh of disbelief. "Um, as much as I want to take a trip to Huxley, how in the world do you expect us to bring back a bunch of people to *West Virginia*? That's not the easiest sell when compared to a city like Huxley. And you know we're just in middle school, right?"

"I do know that." Ani told him. "Young people have a knack for seeing the potential in things. A lot of people lose that as they get older – which is why you all are the perfect candidates to go. You are not tied to jobs, a home, or taking care of a family. And, you can more easily fly under the radar."

"But we still have to convince people to come back." Ali noted. "The city is *huge*. How would we even begin to figure that out?"

"I don't know the city, so I can't tell you the answer to that question." Ani told her. "You will just have to go there and figure it out along the way. And when you find some people who are willing to return, maybe you can take them all back to Orwell on the train. And once you've returned, we can begin to rebuild."

Noah let out a sigh. "Dang it, guys. I don't know…I think I want to check it out. Couldn't hurt to at least try."

Jake jumped a little out of excitement, raising a celebratory fist in victory.

Jake and Noah turned their attention to their friend.

"Ali?" Noah prodded.

"Geez...I don't know!" She strained. "I mean, I want to...but my parents! And we have school!"

"What I'm hearing," Jake said, "is that you *want* to go, but you don't *think* you should go..."

"Yeah..." Ali bashfully looked at the floor.

"I mean, I can't tell you what to do!" Jake was in full salesman mode. "Noah and I can go to Huxley and live it up in luxury all by ourselves, but it would be a lot better if you joined!"

Ali closed her eyes and spent a moment in contemplation, torn between the two options, but her head began to rock back and forth as she talked herself into a decision.

"Okay, okay, okay." Ali reopened her eyes. "I'll go!"

Jake jumped for joy again. "Yippee!" He yelled.

Ali laughed at his pureness.

"BUT." Ali changed her laugh to a serious face while pointing a finger at Jake. "We only go for a couple days. Then we come back. Okay? I don't want my family worrying about me like I've been worried about you all this time."

"Fine by me!" Jake compromised.

Noah turned to speak to Ani. "Okay, Mothman." He said. "We're going to Huxley. What's the next step? Like, how in the world are we supposed to get there?"

"It would be easiest if you took the train." The Mothman told the kids. "That's pretty much the only way to get there, anyway. And the safest."

"Yeah, I agree." Noah returned. "But we don't have any tickets...or any money to *buy* tickets."

"What if you snuck onto the train?" Ani inquired.

"Oh boy, I don't know." Noah answered, scratching the back of his head. "They always have a guard on the boarding platform, don't they? Feels a bit too risky for my blood..."

"The next train leaves tomorrow at 10 a.m." Ani stated. "Don't worry about the guard. I can help with that. If you get in a position to sneak on, I'll distract them for enough time to get you boarded."

Jake began to squirm a bit. "Guys, I'm nervous but excited. I think this is gonna be fun!"

Noah and Ali couldn't help but smile at Jake's unbreakable enthusiasm.

"Get some rest." Ani told the kids. "I will see you in the morning."

"Okay." Noah gave a salute to the Mothman. "It was nice meeting you."

"Same." Ani replied. "And thank you. It was nice to meet you all."

Noah, Jake, and Ali walked over to the door. Peering out, they saw the moon was lighting up the field back to Ali's house. It felt like they had just left a fever dream. As Ali and Noah stepped outside, Jake stayed near the door.

"Jake, aren't you coming?" Ali asked.

"No." He replied. "If I come back now, there's going to be a big fuss. I'll see you tomorrow at the station."

Ali paused for a second before understanding Jake's reasoning, then said, "Okay, stay safe. Goodnight, Jake."

"Goodnight, everyone." He replied.

Ali and Noah didn't talk on the walk back to her house. It was so quiet. They couldn't begin to know what to say about what just happened to them – or what they agreed to. After a while, they reached her backyard.

"Can I sleep on your couch?" Noah asked.

"You worried about your dad?" Ali returned.

"Yeah..." Noah replied.

"Sure." Ali said, understanding. "We need as much sleep as we can get. Tomorrow's a big day."

"Yeah, I don't know how we're supposed to sneak onto a train, but I'm really excited to see Huxley, if we can make it..."

"Me too. I guess we'll figure out the details in the morning."

"Yeah, we will. I'm just glad to know Jake's okay."

"Yeah, me too." Ali turned the knob to the house's side door as they both walked quietly into her house, trying to calm down a sleepy but excited Roxy dog.

"Hi, Roxy." Ali whispered, wrapping the little pit bull in a big hug. "It's time for bed."

She stood up and addressed Noah.

"There are spare blankets and pillows in the closet." She said. "You good?"

"Yeah, I'll figure it out." He whispered. "Thanks again."

"Of course." She whispered back. "Goodnight, Noah."

"Goodnight, Ali." Noah watched as Ali began making her way up the stairs, Roxy following at her heels. He grabbed a blanket and some pillows and stretched out on the couch, replaying the night's events in his mind until he drifted off into sleep.

CHAPTER THREE
TRAIN TO HUXLEY

Ali woke up around five in the morning, trapped in some limbo between nervousness and excitement surrounding her forthcoming adventure. She was especially paranoid about sneaking onto the train, considering her wide-spread reputation for being a goody-two-shoes. For her, jumping a train was like going from zero to one hundred on the badness scale.

The anticipation was making her restless. She kept tossing and turning, trying to go back to sleep, but it wasn't working. She didn't want to get up and start moving around, because she was afraid the noise would wake up Noah. Instead, she just sat in her own dread, hoping to hear a noise come from downstairs that indicated that her friend was awake. Unfortunately for her, that noise never came. So, around nine in the morning, she gave up and slowly crept out of her room and down the carpeted stairs. When she was far enough down the staircase, she leaned her head around the railing and found Noah, still in her house, awake, and staring down at the coffee table.

"Hey. You good?" She asked.

Noah looked up at her. "Yeah, I'm good." He answered, half out of it. "I've been up for a couple hours."

"Me too. Do you still want to go?"

"Yeah...I think so. I think I'll kick myself later on if I don't."

"Yeah, I'm feeling the same way." She hung onto the railing, waiting to see if there was anything else left to cover. "Well, I'm going to go get ready. It'll be about thirty minutes. Need anything?"

"Nah, I'm alright." Noah replied. "Thank you."

"Okay, I'll be right back." She hurried back up the stairs.

"Actually, Ali!" He yelled up to her. She stopped on a dime.

"Yeah?"

"Send Roxy down if she's awake."

"Got it."

Ali cracked open her bedroom door and walked into the bathroom.

Noah called upstairs for Roxy and, after a low and slow stretch, Roxy came fumbling down the stairs, excited to see her friend.

• • • • • • • • •

The train was already at the station when they arrived and was looking as rough as ever. It was so old that it was basically a relic – an old coal-fired train that was painted red and black and sported an iron balcony on its caboose. Every few seconds, it would release some pressurized air, adding a little sound to the otherwise quiet surroundings.

The station sat in a barren valley, save for a few trees that were purposely planted around the building years ago. There wasn't much to see – the entire structure consisted of two brick-walled bathrooms and a gate that led out to the platform. There was no enclosed area dedicated for people to wait on the train indoors – that is, unless they wanted to hang out in the restroom.

Above the gate was a sign that said 'Orwell', and beneath it sat a ticket kiosk where a family of three was trying to buy their passes to the Great City. The family was made up of an old woman, her husband, and a person who seemed to be their daughter.

Ali realized it would be difficult to sneak past the gate where the ticket person was since there was hardly a soul around to blend in with. Instead, she figured it would be easier for her and Noah to go around the station completely and make their approach from the side. She gestured for Noah to keep quiet and follow her, and that's exactly what he did. They made their way down the road and continued walking past the station. As soon as they were out of eyesight of the ticket seller, they cut toward the left bathroom building and squeezed in between the landscaping and the wall, slowly crouch-walking toward the train's platform.

As they reached the back of the building, Ali leaned her head around the corner to observe the situation.

"Only one guard." She whispered. "And the ticket guy at the kiosk."

"Not too bad." Noah confirmed. "But I still don't know how we're supposed to hop on this train without catching anyone's attention."

"Hey, is that Brenda's son?" Jake asked from a shrub behind them, scaring both of his friends.

"Oh my god, Jake." Noah whispered aggressively. "How long have you been there?"

"I got here like five minutes ago. Clearly better at hiding than you all, too. You walked right by me."

"Oh hush." Ali said.

Jake laughed. "I was just giving you a hard time. But seriously, isn't that Brenda's son over there? I think his name is Jeremy."

"Are you sure?" Noah leaned around the corner to see what his friend was talking about. He took a look at the guard and retreated back to his hiding spot.

"I don't think so. Looks a lot like Jeremy though. Except he's too young."

"Oh oh oh...that must be Johnny Wayne, then." Jake figured.

"Oh yeah, Johnny Wayne!" Noah whispered loudly in discovery.

"Didn't he drop out of high school last year?" Jake asked. "I remember somethin' about his girlfriend getting pregnant."

"Yeah, yeah, yeah...that's it." Noah responded. "I guess he's workin' as a guard now."

"I suppose so." Jake returned.

"Is this really our major concern right now?" Ali quietly snapped at the boys.

"I mean, to me it was..." Jake said, backing off. "Y'all need to loosen up a bit. We're going to be fine."

As he said that, the train's engine started.

"Huxley!" Johnny Wayne uttered, somewhat unenthusiastically. "All aboard for Huxley..."

The old couple and their daughter began walking toward one of the train cars.

"This is our chance." Ali determined.

"Not yet." Jake hesitated. "Ani told us he would give us a distraction."

"Ani?" Ali asked.

"Yeah, the Mothman."

"Oh, right. Sorry, I forgot his name."

They waited there on the side of the wall as the family boarded the train. Noah and Ali's impatience continued to build to its limit. Both of them felt that they were about to miss their opportunity to make a break for it.

After all the passengers were settled in their seats, Johnny Wayne closed the doors to each car and signaled to the conductor that the train was ready to make its way down the tracks.

"Okay, enough is enough." Ali said with determination. "We have to go now or we'll miss it."

"Come on, guys." Jake complained. "Y'all need to trust me here. Have a little faith, why don't ya?"

Ali let out a big puff of stress-induced air as she attempted to calm herself down, but it wasn't helping much. She looked again toward the platform. The train's engine was growing louder. It would surely take off at any moment.

Johnny Wayne turned his back to the train and began walking toward the kiosk where the ticket seller was. As he neared the booth, having almost left the platform completely, a rumble of thunder sounded in the distance behind the train. Johnny twisted his back to look behind him, confused as to where the thunder could have come from, given how clear the skies were that day.

Jake's lips formed a slight grin, knowing his patience and trust in his friend Ani had paid off.

Johnny Wayne walked back onto the platform and began a visual inspection of the sky. He noticed only a couple clouds, both of which were small and white and nowhere near the station. He put a hand up to his brow to block the sun so he could see better, and as he did, a large, shadowy mass whipped by him at such a great speed that it knocked him on his butt. The trees and hedges that surrounded the building began to sway heavily from the huge gusts of wind. Ali grabbed her head in an attempt to control her hair.

The ticket seller ducked under the kiosk, trying to hide from the creature. Johnny Wayne struggled to stand up, but just as he began to lift himself off the ground, the dark mass whipped by him again, causing him to fall back down. This time, he just assumed a guarded position, unsure of how to respond to this force of nature.

The children watched as the Mothman ascended into the sky above them, circling the station like a bird of prey. After taking a two-lap assessment of the surrounding area, the soaring creature tucked its wings and performed a free-fall dive toward the station. It fell incredibly fast and seemed like it would plummet directly into the platform at any moment, but just before it reached the tops of the buildings, the monster whipped its wings outward, breaking its momentum, as it used its talons to cling onto the metal archway. The metal 'Orwell' sign creaked from the pressure of the landing as the cursed thunder god stood perched high above the concrete platform – its shadow casting directly over the terrified security guard.

Johnny looked up at the thing in horror. The sun was eclipsing the beast, but he could still see the Mothman's menacing red eyes glowing through the dark aura. He began to shiver as a cold feeling crept up his back. He felt as if Death itself was upon him.

· · · ● · ● · · ·

"This is our chance...go, go, go!" Jake quietly commanded. The three kids took off running past the restroom wall and along the sides of the elevated platform where Johnny was lying.

The train had just started moving away from the station, but it was picking up speed. Ali, Jake, and Noah tried to make up for this by running faster. Ali reached the caboose first and grabbed the railing, finding a secure spot to place her feet. Noah caught up quickly and grabbed onto the balcony soon after. They pulled themselves up and over the rails, then turned back to Jake, who was beginning to lag behind.

"Come on, dude!" Noah directed.

Jake was keeping up okay but was clearly unsure about how he was supposed to leap onto the moving train, especially at his height.

Ali held out her arms over the railing. Noah followed in suit.

"Come on." Ali encouraged. "You got this."

Jake lowered his head and mustered a burst of running energy that managed to bring him much closer to the caboose. He reached out and grabbed onto his friends' arms. Ali and Noah leaned their weight backwards, pulling their friend up and onto the outer side of the railing, where Jake was finally able to slide his feet in between the rails, grab ahold of the horizontal bar for support, and catch his breath.

"Shoot." He uttered in a short breath. "I thought for a second there that y'all were gonna have to go on without me."

"Have a little faith, why don't ya?" Ali sassily joked, repeating his own words back to him.

Jake formed an exhausted smile and surrendered to her wit.

· · · ● · ● · · · ·

Back at the station, Johnny Wayne was still on his butt, frozen in terror from the red-eyed stare.

"Johnny Wayne." The Mothman's voice spoke with authority in the guard's mind. "Do you love your baby's mother?"

"Y.... y.... yes." Johnny could barely get the word out. "Yessir."

"Good. Cherish her and your newborn daughter. Promise me you will do right by them."

Johnny Wayne, with the fear of God in him, nodded his head, confirming he had understood the monster's request.

"Family can take many forms, but they always come first. Don't forget that, Johnny."

"I won't, sir." Johnny Wayne said, trembling and scared out of his mind. "I promise."

Ani stood up straight. "Then my business here is finished."

"But..." Johnny mumbled. "How did you know all that stuff about me?"

The Mothman folded his wings back and bent his broken legs into a crouched position, still clinging onto the metal sign.

"Don't worry Johnny. Life's full of questions. But the good news is...you don't need answers for everything. Take care, buddy."

With one push, the storied creature launched himself off of the sign and into the sky at an unbelievable speed. The takeoff caused a crack of thunder to ripple out in all directions, blowing dust everywhere and ripping the leaves off the trees. Johnny struggled to stand as he watched the half moth, half man soar away from him and in the direction of the train, which was now far away from the platform and moving at full speed.

· · · · ● · ● · · · ·

The kids watched the incredible takeoff from a distance. It almost felt like watching a rocket launch in a way. They all gazed up in awe of the monster's speed as it made its way toward them.

"Guys, here he comes!" Jake yelled in childlike wonder.

Ani caught up to the train in no time and zoomed right over their heads. He circled back into their view, glided for a moment where they could see him, then gave them a wave.

All three friends waved back at him. Ali yelled out a 'thank you!' as their friend swooped down a few feet in the air and let out one final thunderous crack of his wings, propelling him into the horizon.

"Holy cow." Noah said, feeling lucky to have seen something so magnificent. "Look at him go."

· · · ● · ● · · · ·

Back at the station, Johnny Wayne was watching the Mothman disappear into the distance. Once it was clear the creature wasn't returning, he let out a deep sigh of relief and turned to look at the ticket person, who was still hiding behind the kiosk, but who was also peering around the corner to see what was going on.

"Well, thanks for nothin', I guess!" Johnny Wayne complained loudly to his coworker. "Just wanted to leave me out there to fend for myself, huh?"

"If you think I was gonna leave this booth to help you, you got another thing comin'." The seller replied. "Also, and there's no judgment from me, here, but it looks like you've had a spill downstairs."

Johnny looked down, realizing he had peed himself, and let out a sigh. "Well, shoot." He said. "Can you cover for me?"

"Sure."

The soiled guard looked back up and pointed a finger toward the ticket stand. "Hey, you better hope it don't come for you next." He warned. Johnny turned back around and tried to find the Mothman in the horizon, but the monster was long gone. He let out another sigh, dusted his shirt off, clocked out, and left the station. As he got into his car, a notion passed into his mind that he should probably take his family out to a nice dinner.

· · · ● · ● · · · ·

"Gah, that was so cool!" Jake remarked, turning toward his friends on the back of the train. "Did you see how fast he was flying?! That had to be like 80, 90 miles an hour!"

"I've never seen nothin' like it." Ali added, as she watched her hometown fade into the distance. "My heart hasn't rushed like that in so long."

"Same." Jake replied. "Mine's still going!"

There was a pause. All three friends were enjoying their view.

Ali turned her head toward the others. "So...how long until we get there?"

"About two hours, more or less." Noah answered.

"Huh, okay. That's not too bad." She figured. "Now let's just hope this train doesn't fall apart before we get there."

Noah let out a quick laugh. "Ha! Yeah...good luck with that."

They all stood in silence on the back of the train and watched the nearly lifeless valley get smaller and smaller as they entered the West Virginia hills.

As they traveled further into the wilderness, the three friends became sub-jected to more and more of the beautiful scenery Appalachia had to offer – picturesque landscapes of red, orange, and yellow leaves, dense woods filled with all sorts of animals, and peaceful little creeks running through the cool, shaded woods. It felt magical, in a way, so much different from the dirty, concrete-slab-of-a-town they were used to.

About ninety minutes into their train ride, the surrounding mountains began to slope down as they entered an open clearing. The train had passed into a ravine and began to cross through it on the longest and largest bridge they had ever seen. The bridge was so high up, it made the massive river below looked tiny in comparison. The ravine stretched into the distance beyond them for what looked like miles.

"Oh my goodness, y'all." Ali said, staring at the engineering marvel beneath them. "This is the Great Bridge...I remember this! From our West Virginia History class!"

"Is it really?!" Jake asked, gazing down the tracks at the gorgeous burgundy steel structure that anchored itself into the sides of the ravine. "Woah, I think you're right. I guess I never knew just how gigantic it actually is. The pictures they show us are always so far away."

While the kids were looking down at the bridge, they noticed a hawk soaring beneath them. It weaved through the crossed beams and passed into the open air. They followed its path as it flew down the ravine, following the river that ran below it. The hills on either side rolled out so far that it seemed they could go on forever. It was like gazing at an ocean of trees, and the hills were the waves.

"I think this is the most beautiful thing I have seen in my entire life." Noah said, announcing what everyone else was already feeling internally.

The other two nodded in agreement, holding the silence so they could not miss a second of taking in the sight that sat before them.

The train finally cleared the bridge and the ravine, traveling back into the winding hills that blocked the horizon and their view.

"Wow." Ali uttered, still affected by what she had seen.

"Yeah..." Jake agreed, not sure what words could do it justice.

"I'm kind of mad I've never seen that before." Ali said. "Like, it's not that far away."

"It's because nobody freaking goes anywhere most of the time." Jake replied. "That's why I've been trying to get out and explore. This state is like a treasure trove of places that are just...peaceful."

Noah chuckled. "That's ironic."

"What do you mean?"

"I mean..." Noah paused, trying to find the right wording. "We've got places of immense peace in our backyard, while most of the people we know are in a constant state of non-peace, ya know?"

"Yeah, I see that." Ali agreed. "You mean, like, they're restless."

"Yeah. Like why can't we just go out to places like this and chill out? There's so much sadness and worry back home. People keep turning to alcohol or drugs or...whatever...trying to find peace with where they're at, but like...the peace is literally sitting right in our backyard."

"Dang, dude." Jake said.

"I'm sorry." Noah continued. "I think I'm just tired of everyone being all wound up all the time. I literally can't turn on the news without hearing about like fifty things that went wrong each day. Everyone says money is tight, but the funny thing is that nobody around us is even that worried about money or relationships half the time because they're in such a state of panic over global politics or religion, as if they had any say in those matters."

Noah leaned over the railing and had a spark in his eye, like he was envisioning something.

"If we could all just sit out on that bridge for a second...if we could just turn the TVs off and just focus on what was right in front of us...I bet so much of that worry would just wash away."

"Man, I'm with ya." Jake said. "And who knows...maybe if we stick around and be good examples for everyone, we can move toward that place you're dreaming of."

"Yeah...I don't know." Noah hesitated.

"What's wrong?" Jake asked. "You don't want to?"

"I do." Noah let out a big breath. "I just don't know if I belong here. Like, long term, ya know?"

"Well sure ya do." Ali added. "We love having you here."

"Yeah, I know..." Noah understood. "It's not that." He paused. "It's more about my dad, I think."

Ali and Jake were silent. They didn't know how to address the topic.

"Every time I'm home, I'm in fear." Noah said. "I'm in fear because everything could be fine at one moment and then completely turn on its head at the flip of a switch...and in the case of my dad, the switch is just completely...random."

"I'm sorry, Noah." Ali put an arm around her friend and tried to comfort him. "You'll be out of the house in just a few years, though. After that, you can do whatever you want. We can all get a place together! That would be fun."

"Thanks, guys." Noah responded. "I love you all, but I just don't know if I can stay in a town that I have such a negative history with. I kind of want to start new someplace else. Like, as soon as we're out of high school, I'd like to travel around and find somewhere that's a better fit for me."

Jake was hurt by Noah's last sentence. All Jake ever wanted was to have his friends together in the place that he loved. The idea that his friendship wasn't enough for Noah hurt him to his core.

Ali, on the other hand, was sitting in a bit of an existential whirlwind. She had never considered life outside of her town before. She had always been comfortable with where she was. She loved her family, her dog, and her best friends, but this idea that someplace might be a better fit for her, like, specifically *for* her, introduced a bit of unease in her mind.

"Well," Ali started, "I propose that the three of us go on even more adventures after this. See all we can see. Both in the state and out. I assume that's the only way we're going to find out what's actually right for us, anyhow."

Jake's hurt continued to grow more and turned into frustration. "Why do you all have this need to leave all of the sudden?" He asked harshly. "Noah, I get that your home life sucks, and I don't want to downplay that, but can't we just all stay together and enjoy what's around us?"

"I just don't think it's that easy, dude." Noah said.

"It is for me…" Jake replied.

"I know." Noah looked down, scared that he was causing his friend pain. "But it's hard for me to imagine staying in a place that hurts me every time I lower my guard. And no amount of pretty bridges are going to fix that, either."

"But…what about me?" Jake asked. "I don't want to go anywhere else."

"I don't know, man…we might just have to cross that road when we get there…"

Ali was saddened by the conversation. She understood both of her friends' arguments and agreed with each of them in her own way. Sticking around and spending a lifetime with the people you grew up with – the people who knew you in and out and who would always love you no matter what – was such a comforting idea; but the idea of getting out and seeing all that one could be – even finding a place that melded better with one's own interests and desires – sounded like a life that could be full of adventure and discovery. Both ideas were romantic in their own way, but Ali wasn't sure which held higher favor in her mind.

The conversation left the adventurers in a sort-of stalemate. Nobody felt like they could say anything that would bring the other person to their side. After all, they were speaking from what they knew, and what someone knows is inherently limited to their own experiences. If another person hasn't shared that same experience, how could they understand what it was like? Instead of risking further instability, the three friends just opted to stay in silence, choosing temporary peace over a fight for understanding.

This awkwardness continued for a while until the train approached a dark tunnel made of moss-covered stone. A rusty metal sign next to it said

Now Leaving: West Virginia. It was at this moment that their trip became suddenly real to them. Whether they wanted to or not, they were going to have to leave their comfort zones and explore something entirely unfamiliar to them. Nobody else knew where they were, and the kids had no way to contact help if it was needed. From this point, they were completely on their own.

Noah, Jake, and Ali watched as the train passed into the carved-out mountain. Inside, the temperature was much cooler. It was weirdly comforting to be in there, too, despite the darkness. Occasionally, a little glimmer of light would reflect off the moisture in the cave, revealing the wet and jagged stone walls. Everything smelled so clean in there, like it was a place that was entirely detached from the outside world.

They took in the entire experience until the train exited the other side of the tunnel and abruptly flooded them once again with light and greenery galore. The tracks immediately pulled them around a bend, and the train began to run parallel to a massive concrete structure that stood in the distance.

The colossal concrete giant that sat before them had walls over 50 stories high that bore a ruffled and also-concrete dome on top of it. It was truly a marvel of engineering, something that didn't exist anywhere else in the world. There were thick electrical lines that ran up its sides, and at the very top of the dome, beams of multi-colored light danced in the sky.

"Guys, what is that?" Ali asked. "It's freaking huge."

"If we're taking bets?" Jake offered up. "I'd have to bet that's Huxley."

"Jesus."

"Yeah…"

"The whole city is in there?"

"Pretty sure."

"Gah...lee. Aren't they afraid it's gonna collapse?"

"I'm sure they've thought that through. This place is no joke."

"What's that thing hovering in the lights at the top?"

"What do you mean?"

"Look, up there. Do you see it? It's like a torch or something."

"Maybe some sort of beacon?"

"Maybe..."

As the three friends had their eyes fixed on the sky, they witnessed a storm cloud quickly materialize over the city.

"Y'all...did you see that?"

"Sure did. Never seen a cloud form that fast."

"What in the world is going on?"

"Look, the torch is moving up toward the cloud."

"I am so confused right now."

"It's getting higher."

"There is seriously only that cloud in the sky and nothing else? Where did it come from?

"Guys…"

"What?"

"I think I know what it is."

"What is it?"

A lightning bolt shot out of the cloud and struck the torch-looking object. All three of the kids, who were so focused on that point, were jump scared and let out a short shout.

"Gosh, that scared the crap out of me."

A lightning bolt struck the thing again. And again. And again.

"Guys!" Jake shouted as they all averted their eyes at the incoming light flashes. "It's gotta be her!"

"Are you sure?!" Noah shouted back.

Suddenly, a stillness washed over the sky. The lightning strikes stopped. The kids quickly looked back up above the dome and saw that the figure was now surrounded by an aura of energy stetching fifty feet in all directions. Beautiful strands of electricity swirled around it in a massive orb of controlled power.

"Hey Noah."

"Yeah?"

"Disregard my last question. It's definitely her."

As he said that, the massive orb of electricity funneled into a dense beam of energy that shot downward toward the city, blinding the entire sky in light.

"Get down!"

The air around them vibrated from the blast as the kids ducked away to guard themselves against the waves of heat that were emanating from the electric pulse.

They maintained their guarded position until the cool fall air returned. When they looked back at the city, the electrical cords that ran along the city's walls were completely illuminated, as if they had stored all the energy that was sent toward them.

"Woah."

"Did that, like, charge them?"

"I think so."

"Where do they run?"

The train turned away from its parallel line with the city and began moving straight for the domed enclosure.

"I guess we're about to find out..."

Ali felt a jittery feeling come over her.

"Guys, I'm nervous."

"How come?"

"What if they catch us?"

"Well, I guess it'll be a short stay, then."

They shared a brief laugh.

"Should we come up with a game plan?"

"Nah, just go with the flow. It'll be alright. As far as they know, we're here for the exact same reason as that family inside."

"Right. Okay."

The caboose passed through Huxley's outer walls, and a large black gate closed behind them.

"Well y'all. It just got mega real. We're officially in Huxley."

Chapter Four

Huxley: The Great City

As the train screeched to a stop outside the domed city, the children ran inside the train car to join the three passengers who boarded in Orwell. There was a welcoming party awaiting their arrival. A mustachioed man stood in the front of the group, wearing a top hat and a white three-piece suit with ornate golden embroidery. He lifted his cane off the ground and stepped forward.

"Good evening, travelers!" The man held up a hand in greeting and then placed it back on the top of his cane. "Welcome to Huxley, the Greatest City on Earth. I am the head marshal, Marshall! Yes, you heard that right. I'm here to introduce you to the city and answer any questions you might have. Now, would the six of you fine people enjoy taking a little tour of our marvelous metropolis?"

"Oh...yes please!" The old woman from Orwell answered, very sweetly, as her daughter helped her step off the train.

"Terrific! Well, if everyone is on board for the tour, we'll be heading right this way!" Marshal Marshall said with entertaining enthusiasm as he spun on one leg, balancing with his cane, and began leading the group inside the city's walls.

The interior of Huxley's humongous dome was filled with large glass buildings and gigantic billboards. The children gazed in wonder at all the lights and grandeur above them. The colors from the LED screens danced on the whole town. There were all-glass elevators traveling up and down the concrete walls. Everywhere the group looked, they saw a sign for more and more spectacular events – plays, dances, movies, comedy shows, sports games, circuses – anything the mind could imagine. The children were so captivated by all of these attention-grabbing displays that they weren't paying a lick of attention to anything the marshal was saying on their tour – that is, until Ali accidentally ran right into the back of the old woman who was walking in front of her, causing the woman to trip forward. The woman's daughter and husband caught her before she fell, and Ali went on to apologize three separate times, to which the woman assured her everything was okay. The event brought the marshal's words back into focus.

"Next up is one of our most proud achievements...the vertical farms!" Marshall guided the tour's attention to a group of large glass containers, stacked on top of each other, that raised all the way up as far as the eye could see. "With this system, spearheaded by our innovative founder, we have been able to produce 300% more food than the need of our residents. They never have to worry about food again!"

"Woah." Noah reacted with his head tilted all the way back, his eyes gazing up at the seemingly endless food supply.

"Woah is right!" Marshall said. "These farms actually run on 98% less water than traditional farming. Can you believe that?"

"That's amazing." The old man commented. He couldn't believe his eyes or ears. An oversupply of food was something he had never heard of.

Sometimes, when he was growing up, when times were tough, all his mom would give him to eat was a slice of bread with some sugar on it. And now, there was an overabundance of healthy options for *everyone* in this city. He smiled at the thought of all the people in the following generations who wouldn't have to go through what he did.

"You know somethin'." The old man started, wagging a contemplative finger at the farms. "I bet this thing doesn't have any bug problems, either."

"You're exactly right, sir." Marshall confirmed. "And that is why there's no need for us to use pesticides or any other chemicals like that to preserve the crops. Nope, they just grow out of the cells and we eat them, just like it's supposed to be."

"Who maintains all of this?" Noah asked, seeing this as a massive under-taking.

"Well, the people of Huxley, of course!" Marshall answered. "We have vertical farmers, bioengineers, and electricians who work together to keep these things runnin'! It's all under a very efficient process."

"But...I'm confused." Jake butted in.

"What's your question, son?" Marshall asked.

"Those types of jobs require a lot of money." Jake proceeded. "And like, I absolutely see that you all have no shortage of money. But, like, where does the money to do something like this come from? Government grants?"

"No, sir." The marshal said. "It's all paid for in-house."

"But...how?" Jake pressed on.

"Did you see those big electrical wires on the city's walls on your way in?"

"Yeah."

"Well, that's how we do it!" The marshal explained. "Huxley has access to a wealth of electrical power, which we farm, sell, and distribute to the local towns and cities, putting all the revenue back into improving our home...and improved it we have!"

"Yeah, I'll say." The old woman's daughter spoke up. "This tour has already blown me away, and we've only been here for like twenty minutes."

"Well, let's keep going, then!" Marshall said. "There's so much more to see."

As they continued on their walk, Ali saw a billboard for Huxley University.

"Sir, is that university expensive to go to?" She asked Marshall. "My mom says she wants me to go to a university, and I'm only about to enter high school, but I would love to stop by and check it out since I don't know how many chances I'll have by then."

"We can absolutely stop by good ole HuxU if everyone is okay with it." Marshall said. "And to answer your question, Huxley is actually *free* to attend for *any* citizen of the city. So if you would like to move here before college to take advantage of that deal, it would definitely be a good consideration!"

"Are you serious?" Ali couldn't believe what she heard. "Y'all can do free college too? You must be selling a lot of electricity." As the words left her mouth, she caught how obvious she had just sounded. The city clearly had an unlimited supply of electricity in the form of their lightning bug goddess founder. If Nimkii could produce charges like they saw a few minutes ago regularly, it was no surprise that Huxley had so much money on hand.

"We get by pretty well, I admit." The marshal told her. "But yes, I'm very serious! Please consider attending. It's truly a fantastic place to receive an education. Would the rest of you like to see the university during the tour?"

"Well, I'm sure it's very nice," the old woman began, "but I'm too old to worry about such things. Is there any place else you would recommend we visit?"

"Absolutely, ma'am." Marshall replied. "Would you like to check out our community center? There are tons of great senior events there. Swimming, bridge, billiards, checkers, you name it! It would be a great place to meet people, too."

"Is it okay if we go there?" The old woman asked her daughter. "I'd like to take a look at it."

"Of course, mom." The daughter replied, resting a hand on her mother's shoulder.

"Okay." The woman said with a smile on her face. "We would like to see the community center instead, if that's okay."

"That'll be no problem at all!" Marshal verified. "Let me get another tour guide to meet us in a few minutes and that way everyone can see what they want to see."

Marshal Marshall whipped out a comm device and called for another tour guide to meet them at what he called 'Station 16'.

"Alright, one more stop, and then we'll split off for a bit." He told the group, turning around and pointing his cane into the sky. "This way!"

The group walked through the city for a few more minutes until they reached a massive courtyard in the center of the town. A colossal green turf stretched out for at least two acres, with bikers and runners circumnavigating the area. Inside, there were people reading, playing frisbee, and generally relaxing about the space. Light towers, scattered throughout the park, illuminated the turf below.

"This is so fancy!" The old woman's daughter noted. "We don't have anything like this back home. You could have a good time out here at any time of the day...or heck, even at night!"

"That's right." The marshal said. "But *this* is actually why I brought you here." He led them over to a machine inside the park. "Take a look at this." He said as he pushed a button and water began to flow out of the machine.

"Here's something you've probably never encountered before." Marshall continued. "Free, public, tap water. But wait! It's filtered. Not just carbon filters...nope. The works! Sediment, lead, reverse osmosis...the whole she-bang! It runs through every pipe in the city, it has been rated the *cleanest* water in Appalachia, and it doesn't cost the residents a *dime*. Doesn't that just blow your mind?"

Jake was really stunned by this display. "It...does, actually." He answered, feeling a sense of meaning come across him, like he had just discovered what it was like to see something both cool and useful. He thought about all the chemical leaks, boil water advisories, and main breaks he had experienced in his short lifetime. That was a *real* problem in his home state, and here Huxley had used modern technology, ingenuity, and collaboration to solve the very problem he had seen so much of. He felt a deep inspiration from it all. "This is amazing, sir." He told the tour guide. "Have you had any problems with runoff from the mines or chemical leaks or anything like that? It's really bad for us back home."

"Oh heavens, no!" Marshall responded. "Our Executive Board that oversees the region won't let anything like that near our water supply."

"Geez." Jake scratched his head. "I ain't ever seen a place that didn't have water troubles."

Just then, a woman drove up in an electric golf cart.

"Ah, Sara!" Marshall exclaimed. "Great timing. These three lovely folks would like to see the community center." He gestured toward the old couple and their daughter.

"Wonderful!" Sara responded. "I'm happy to give you a ride there and anywhere else you'd like to go."

"Thank you, ma'am." The old woman's daughter said as she helped her parents into the back of the golf cart.

"Are you all going somewhere else?" Sara asked Marshall.

"Yes!" He answered. "I'm going to give the little ones a tour of the university."

"Got it." Sara replied. "You all have fun!" She stepped into the driver's seat of the golf cart.

"One more thing before you all go." Marshall said to the older trio. "I have a surprise for you later today in the same courtyard that we just came from, so meet me there at 5 p.m. sharp!"

The three of them nodded to acknowledge what he said.

"You all go have fun, now!" He tapped the top of the cart and the other half of the group headed off toward the community center.

"Alright, you three." Marshall turned his attention back to the kids and kicked his cane loose from the ground, holding it high in the sky once again. "To the university!"

They walked through the city for a while until they reached one of the elevators situated along the city's wall. Marshall punched in a code on the elevator's keypad, and the doors slid open. When the group was fully inside the elevator, a soft orange light kicked on and a female voice spoke through the speakers, "Hello, Marshall. Where are we going today?"

"The university, Penny. Thank you!" He said.

A pleasant tone sounded, indicating that Penny had received the request. The elevator began raising the group high above the city. Relaxing lo-fi music faded in as the lights inside the elevator dimmed, allowing for optimal viewing of the magnificent city below them.

About a third of the way up the wall, Ali noticed a video game tournament taking place on one of Huxley's many levels. There was a huge screen with stage lights, and the kids could hear roars from the crowd, even inside the elevator.

"Hey, guys!" Ali grabbed their attention. "Look, they're playing our game!" She pointed at the passing scene.

"What?!" Jake said in disbelief. "No way!" He crouched to catch a last glimpse of the action before the elevator traveled too high and the event left their view. He turned to look at Marshall. "Sir, does Huxley do a lot of video game tournaments?"

"Oh, yes, yes, yes. All the time!" Marshall confirmed. "With cool prizes, too!"

"That's sick..." Jake said as he went back into a trance-like stare toward the city, its lights dancing in his eyes. He imagined being on that stage and winning a tournament with his friends, and what it would feel like to have the whole crowd cheering them on.

"What kinds of prizes?" Ali asked.

"Oh, all sorts." Marshall answered. "Money, concerts, nights out on the town. The last prize they gave out was a year-long subscription to the movies!"

"Oh, man. I *love* going to the movies." Ali said as she put her face back against the glass in wonder, getting just as lost in a daydream as Jake was.

"Yeah, movies are awesome." Jake replied from his own wonder.

"What are some of the most popular jobs in the city?" Noah asked, letting his friends soak up their trance. "Surely not everyone can be a fancy garden scientist. I'm sure I'm not even smart enough to know how to grow a normal garden, let alone do something like those vertical farms do."

The elevator slowed down, the music faded, and Penny's orange light grew brighter.

"Welcome to the university level." She said as the doors opened.

"Thank you, Penny." Marshall responded, turning to address the group. "Well, don't worry about that, buddy. There's so much here for you to do. You'll find something that fits you perfectly, I'm sure of it! And we're in just the right place to get started." He began walking out of the elevator. "Come on everybody!"

The group entered a futuristic corridor, all white, that focused on a main desk situated against the back wall of the long, narrow room. Behind the desk was a large 'Huxley University' logo hovering on an LED screen. The tour walked through the spotless walkway until they reached the front desk.

"Hello Marshal Marshall," one of the desk assistants said with a smile. "On another tour?"

"Yes ma'am!" Marshall replied.

"Can I get you all anything while you're walking around?" The woman asked the children.

"Yeah, actually, do you have any coffee?" Ali questioned.

"I'll take a soda, and some snacks, if you have any." Jake added.

Marshall smiled at the young group taking every chance to capitalize on the offer.

"Of course, let me see what I can get for you all." The woman said as she stepped into a back room and emerged a minute later with a coffee, a couple of sodas, and a handful of snacks for the kids.

"Thank you so much!" Ali said. "We literally haven't eaten all day."

"Well no worries at all!" The woman told her. "If you need anything, just let me know."

"Thank you, Rose." Marshall said kindly to the young woman before turning back toward the kids. "Alright, everyone. We're heading this way."

He began walking them down a new hallway. All the doors were closed, and muffled voices could be heard within each room.

"We had this university in mind from the beginning." The marshal explained to the group. "Traditional colleges were a slow, inefficient, burdenous mess. Lazy tenured professors, massive upkeep, heating inefficiencies, and poor learning outcomes most of the time. We fixed all of that with HuxU. One building dedicated to efficient learning. Our students learn so fast here compared to everywhere else that they don't even need to spend but about one, maybe two years on a traditional four-year degree most of the time. And as I mentioned, it's as free as the wind."

"That's an amazing deal." Ali told Marshall.

"Sure is." Marshall replied. "Here, take a look at one of our classes that's in session right now."

He swiped a security card on an electric panel that dissolved the tint on the classroom's window to reveal a live college course that was underway. There was an animated elephant on the screen holding a stick and pointing at what looked like a diagram of a heating and cooling system.

"That's Luna the Elephant." Marshall said. "She's phenomenal. An A.I. that has been fed information from every ivy league university, technical school, and online college in the country. It's amazing to watch her go. She's teaching a class on HVAC units now, but it looks like she has a heliophysics graduate course coming up as soon as it's done. Isn't that something?"

"Yessir, it is." Noah agreed. "So, does that mean I can go here, too, even if I don't want to do normal college stuff?"

"You mean like a trade?" The marshal asked, and after seeing Noah nod his head, said, "Of course, of course! All forms of education are in-house."

"Hey, y'all, maybe that means we can stick together after high school." Noah said to the group. "All three of us can move out here. Jake, you can be close enough to home, I can get out of town, and Ms. Smarty-pants over there can get that fancy degree we all know she wants so bad."

Ali shot a jestful glare in Noah's direction. Marshall let out a chuckle. "I like you all." He said. "Let's head back to the elevators. Do you all need a bathroom break?"

"Oh, yes please." Jake said.

"I could use one, too." Ali seconded.

"Okay, we'll take a stop before we move on." Marshall confirmed.

The group made their way to the restrooms and split off.

As Ali walked into the bathroom, she heard sounds of a girl talking, but nobody was answering. She assumed the girl was talking to someone on the phone.

"Yeah, it was awful." The girl said from inside a stall. "The farm cell on my block just went out yesterday for no reason. I had to go all the way to Sector C just to get vegetables. It took like three extra minutes. Yeah, I know! And then after I submitted a complaint, the maintenance guy came by and asked me if I had any problems with the farm cell in the past. It was so awkward."

Ali wondered what kind of an inconvenience someone would have from a three-minute delay in receiving free fresh produce. It would take at least ten minutes by car just to get to the closest Orwell grocery store, let alone gathering the food, paying for it, and driving back. Ali caught herself judging the one side of the conversation too heavily and decided to join her friends back in the lobby.

"Alright, are we all ready to move on?" Marshall asked as the four of them reconvened. The kids nodded. "Good!" He said. "Now, before we head out, is there anything else you all would like to see?" He checked his watch. "We still have...about three hours before we have to meet the others back in the courtyard."

The three friends looked at each other, checking to see if anyone had any suggestions.

"Do you all have anything?" Jake asked. "Because *I* have something..."

Ali laughed a little. "What is it?"

"Well, I've seen a lot of the ads for Huxley on TV," Jake explained, "and I remember them saying that this place had an indoor roller coaster. Is that still true?"

"Not only is it true, but there's a whole theme park inside of Huxley!" Marshall told them.

"Get the frick out of here." Jake replied.

"I will not!" Marshall said, jokingly. "I like it too much. Would you all like to check it out?"

"Absolutely!" Jake said enthusiastically.

"Wait, guys." Noah held up. "We don't have any money. I only have like twenty bucks on me."

"I have a fifty from my birthday, but that's about it." Ali noted. "Will that be enough to go on a couple rides, Marshall?"

"Have you all seriously been listening to me jabber on about this city all day and not picked up on a theme yet?" Marshall asked.

"It's free, isn't it?" Noah said, understandingly.

"Well, the theme park isn't *totally* free, but admission is." The tour guide replied. "But don't worry about that. Rides and food are on me. This is our courtesy to you for joining us on this tour."

"Are you serious?" Noah asked in disbelief.

"Well, duh!" Marshall responded. "Come on..." They walked into the elevator, and Penny guided it across the city to the theme park.

Once there, Ali, Noah, and Jake had a grand time while the marshal stayed around the front of the park and waited for them to be done. They rode tons of roller coasters, tried out a drop tower, and even went on some kids rides for the heck of it.

Ali bought some deep-fried cookies, Noah a funnel cake, and Jake a mess of hand-dipped corndogs from a huge food stand called Greasy Fingers.

"I think I'm in love." Jake said, sucking the ketchup and mustard off his fingers as they walked back to meet Marshall at the front.

"Here they are!" The marshal exclaimed as the three friends approached him. "You all ready for your final surprise?"

Noah, mouth still full of funnel cake, and with sugar all over his shirt, said, "Yessir we are!"

"Great! Let's do it." Marshall replied as he began leading everyone back toward the elevators.

When the group reached the courtyard, the elderly couple was already there with their daughter, clearly drained from such a long day, not to mention the two-hour train ride this morning.

"Alright, everyone." Marshall said loudly to the reunited tour group. "I'm sure you folks are ready to wrap the day up and get some sleep, but trust me, you don't want to miss this!"

He called in a request on his comm device, and as soon as he did, the platform they were standing on, which was situated in the middle of the courtyard, began lifting them slowly into the air. The sudden movement spooked the group at first, but everyone quickly adjusted to the lifting motion once it was underway.

After raising everyone about twenty-five feet above the courtyard, just high enough to where they could see the city stretching back in the distance, Marshall spoke into his comm device once more.

"We're ready for Nimkii." He said, as the children's eyes grew wide, realizing what was happening.

Two seconds after the words left his mouth, the platform at the top of the dome began to open like a camera shutter, and a fiery figure descended into the city below.

"Uhhh... guys...guys..." Ali tapped the back of her hand on her friends to get their attention, her eyes fixed on the lightning god above.

Select LED screens close by changed to show live camera feed footage of the monster as she slowed her descent into the city, remaining suspended high above the group.

"Ladies and gentlemen," Marshall said, "I would like to introduce you to the woman who has made everything you've seen today possible. The founder of Huxley, the Greatest City on Earth, Nimkii!"

He and the tour guide began to clap, as well as others in the area who were watching Nimkii's appearance.

Seeing her close up, she was every bit how Ani described her. The fire was the dead giveaway, but her fingers were deformed, and her body was trapped in a metal suit that looked as if it had turned green over time, kind of like the Statue of Liberty. Her eyes were covered by goggles that reflected all the dancing lights around her.

"Good evening." Nimkii's voice radiated from the speakers in the court-yard. "I am Nimkii, the founder of the Great City of Huxley. It is a pleasure to meet you all."

The lightning god's presence was overwhelming for the kids. The Moth-man was scary when they met him, but she was otherworldly – a different kind of powerful. Jake felt like she could read every thought he had – that she could see into his soul. After seeing the lightning beam she created outside, the kids all knew the immense power she possessed, and you could hear it in her voice too. They all stood there, awestruck by the spectacle.

"Surely by now," the goddess continued, "you have seen that this place is no ordinary city. This is a wonder of the world – a landmark of human achievement – a place where you can be healthy, financially stable, edu-cated, and given more amenities and luxuries than what all of the towns and cities in this region could offer you combined. This is because Huxley is founded on the idea that we can all live fun, happy, extraordinary lives, free from the suffering, the woes, and the burdens of the typical human experience."

Not a soul in the group moved as these words echoed in their ears. They stood in complete stillness, hanging on to the gravity of each word.

"We believe here that there is no one correct way to live life." She continued. "We believe that each individual has a life that is right for them and them alone. That is why we as a city do not push any agenda, politic, or way of life onto our citizens. Come as you are, stay as you are. And if you need any help creating the life that you dream of, we will do all that we can to see to it that you can achieve that life which you deserve."

The words the kids heard were romantic, but the message didn't feel like a hollow pitch – it actually felt real. It felt believable. And it felt this way because it was clear, just looking around, that everyone was *actually* all the things she was describing – healthy, happy, and enjoying their lives. The idea was hard to conceive, but only because the kids had never seen anything like it before.

"So, please, stay as long as you like." Nimkii wrapped up. "Let us know what your next steps are, and we will see to it that you get there. Thank you again for visiting my city. I am so happy you are here."

As she said that, the nearby citizens began their applause once more. Nimkii levitated up and out of the dome, and once she was out of sight, the dome's platform closed behind her.

"Wasn't that something?!" Marshall asked the group.

"She's incredible!" The old woman's face was full of wonder. "I loved her dress, too."

Marshall laughed a bit, still looking at the top of the dome. "Yes, well, she's certainly a force of nature." He turned around to face everyone. "Now! I'm sure you all have had a long day and want to rest up. Would you prefer to sleep on the train ride back to your towns, or would you like to stay the night in one of our hotels?"

All six members of the tour unanimously agreed to stay the night in the hotel. It was a no-brainer for the kids, who had just experienced the most fun day of their lives. They felt totally free, like a whole new world of possibility had opened up to them.

"Terrific!" Marshall enthused. "Now, for those of you that can pay for our hotel, just a heads up, the room fee is $150 a night. Now, I know that may be out of the realm of possibility for a few of you, but don't worry, if you're financially strained, we *do* have a program that will let you stay the night here for free."

"What's the program?" The old woman's daughter asked the marshal.

"It's a 1-for-1 program." He went on. "One night in the hotel for one volunteer shift during the day, doing things like cleaning up the parks or helping out the city in some way. We have a list of options you can pick from – all of them relatively simple tasks – just one of the many ways we try to maintain the city while being fair to all."

"Oh, well that doesn't sound too bad." The daughter said, turning to her parents. "Mom, are we able to cover the cost of the hotel? I don't mind taking a shift for you and Dad so you all don't have to worry about workin' or nothin'."

"We're not worried, dear." Her mother sweetly replied. "Your father and I are going to cover the cost of the two rooms – one for you, and one for your father and me. We've budgeted enough for that."

Her daughter smiled and gave her a hug. "Thank you both."

"Okay, so we have three people paying." Marshall calculated. "How about you, young ones? Remember, if you don't want to pick up the shift, you can absolutely take the train back to your hometown, free of charge."

The three friends silently, through facial expressions, communicated that they were okay to take a volunteer shift, especially if it meant staying another day in the city.

"All great." The marshal replied. "Now, Sara, here, will take down your information, give you your hotel room keys, and let you pick your work assignments. If you need anything at all, she's here to help. Sincerely, it has been a great pleasure meeting all of you." Marshall delivered a polite and low theatrical bow to his group.

"Bye, Mr. Marshall!" The kids said. "Thank you!" Everyone waved goodbye to their guide. The marshal tipped his hat, kicked his cane out again, rotated about face, and walked off into the city.

"Marshal Marshall is amazing." Sara addressed the group, holding an electronic tablet in both hands. "Now, if I can just get you all to fill out some quick details for me here, the computer will auto-generate your hotel keys. For the three people choosing to volunteer, you can also select your assignments when you're finished by clicking the option at checkout that says 'Add Volunteer Assignment'".

The old man took the tablet first and began filling in his information.

"This thing is askin' me how long we've been married." He called out to his wife.

"Well, don't you remember?" She asked him.

"Of course I do. 48 years…" He stated, turning around to talk to Sara. "I would've got out in half the time if I had just killed her!" He joked.

Ali chuckled at the statement. So did his wife. The daughter gave him a whack on his back and said 'Dad!' out of embarrassment, but he kept giggling.

"Honey, if you've been going for as long as we have," the old woman said, "you've gotta be able to have a similar sense of humor."

The daughter shook her head at her crazy parents.

The kids were given the tablet after their fellow tourgoers received their hotel keys. For their volunteer assignments, Ali selected the 'Media Department Livestream' option because she thought it would be fun to work with the cameras, and the boys chose an option called 'Eschaton Watch Guard' only on the basis that the name itself sounded cool.

While selecting the guard duty, the boys received a warning on the screen – something about age verification and waivers for injury – but they quickly scrolled through it and hit 'Accept' because they were too sold on the name.

"What's an Eschaton?" Jake asked the general area around him, still studying the tablet.

"It's a city in northern West Virginia." Ali answered.

"Huh, okay. It says here we have to meet our supervisor at the train station at 9 a.m." He looked at Noah. "I guess we're going back to West Virginia after all."

"Perfect, just when I thought I had escaped!" Noah joked awkwardly. "Ali, do you know where your workplace is?"

As he asked that question, Ali began to feel this weird, sinking feeling in her stomach. It was something she had never experienced before, so she couldn't tell what it was or where it came from. She placed a hand on her midsection and looked down.

"You okay, Ali?" Jake asked worriedly.

"Um, I don't know." She said. "Maybe I'm just a little homesick."

"Or maybe you're a little actual sick." Noah responded. "We had *a lot* of carnival food."

She laughed through her discomfort. "Yeah...maybe that's it." She closed her eyes for a second, gathered herself, and reopened them, letting out a deep breath. "Anyway, my shift is at noon. I'll walk around tomorrow and find where it is."

"Okay." Jake said, still a bit worried for her. "It's hard being away from home, but I have to admit, this place is pretty cool, yeah?"

Ali smiled. "It definitely made it a lot easier to be away. It's been, like, the coolest, most incredible day I've ever had."

"Yeah, me too." Noah agreed.

"Same." Jake thirded. "Alright, y'all. Let's get to bed. We've got another big, fun day ahead of us tomorrow."

"That's for sure." Ali turned to start walking. "Can we stop by the vertical farms on the way up? I want to wash out some of this icky feeling I have in my stomach with something that isn't carnival food."

Jake laughed a little. "I mean you can, but don't expect me to join ya! I think I'm gonna go back for Round 2 at Greasy Fingers tomorrow."

"Geez." She was amazed by her friend's appetite. "You're braver than I am."

"Ah, you just gotta build up a tolerance for it." Jake said. "Leave that healthy stuff for the athletes and the hippies."

Ali cracked a smile and shook her head at her goofy friend as the three of them walked off to find an elevator so Penny could take them to their hotel.

HUXLEY
HUXLEY
Hux...
YOUR FU...
AWAITS!
DINING
M

Chapter Five

THE ESCHATON WATCH GUARD

When Noah woke up the next morning, he had that strange feeling one gets when they sleep somewhere unfamiliar, wake up, and don't know where they are. He checked the time. They still had an hour to be at the train station. Noah walked over to the hotel window and opened the curtains, revealing the dazzling metropolitan lights below. The city was still there, still great, and looked exactly the same as it did last night. The lack of sunlight coming into the dome left everything in a very consistent state, and Noah thought about how the city must not ever get any rain, snow, windstorms, or the like. It probably made it easier to keep the city in such a pristine condition, too.

Jake was still fast asleep and needed to be shaken into consciousness. After the boys got showered and dressed, they made their way to the hotel's breakfast bar, which was serving a ham and spinach omelet. They ate it and didn't complain, but Jake found himself daydreaming about having a buttered-up bacon, egg, and cheese breakfast sandwich from his hometown biscuit restaurant.

"What's the point of eating healthy if it kills your spirit?" Jake asked Noah.

"I think it's to feel better in the moment." Noah answered. "Like to have more energy during the day and not be so weighed down."

"The only thing I think people who eat like this are weighed down by is their conscience." Jake stated.

Noah chuckled at Jake's attempt to find profundity in a spinach omelet.

The rest of their breakfast was eaten in silence, and once their plates were clean, the boys made their way to the train depot.

When they got there, a fellow volunteer led them outside to the train platform. Aside from the dense fog that obscured the surrounding area outside the city, the first thing the boys noticed was the train that was set to leave for Eschaton. This was no ordinary train, at least nothing like they were used to. This thing was sleek, modern, and sported a polished chrome finish. The front car on the train looked like an airplane with a long, round nose that swooped downward, designed for optimal aerodynamics. No smokestack, no pressurized air, and no iron balcony on the caboose.

"Okay, Huxley is officially the coolest place, ever." Jake said, walking up to inspect the vehicle.

"Here." The volunteer said to the boys. "You all go ahead and sign in on the tablet, and then feel free to sit anywhere on the train you'd like."

"Wait." Noah said to the man. "We're not even sure what we're supposed to do. What's a watch guard?"

"Oh," the volunteer uttered, looking at his tablet, "I'm not really the person to ask. I'm just here to check everyone in." He scanned his device until he found the information he was looking for and looked back up. "It looks like your supervisor is Captain Balázs, and he's already checked in, so I'm sure he'll tell you what's going on when you get on the train."

"Oh, okay." Noah processed. "Thanks."

"No problem." The volunteer returned. "Here you go." He handed the boys the tablet to sign them in.

When the boys stepped onto the train, it became even more clear that this vehicle was of a caliber they hadn't seen before. Instead of the nasty curtains they were used to on passenger trains, the large windows in this vehicle had electric gel-activated dimmers inside the glass so that each row could customize their level of translucency all the way to zero visibility. The seats were a clean grey leather with heating and cooling pores to adjust seat temperature. On the backs of each seat were mini televisions, donned with charging ports for every device possible. And resting on each seat was a clean, packaged blanket and pillow for optimal resting and relaxation.

"Is it possible to live on a train?" Jake asked in wonder, gliding his hands across every seat as they walked down the aisle, eventually picking one to plop down on. He immediately began playing with all the seat adjustment settings while Noah sat down in the seat across the aisle from him.

"Man." Jake said, reclining his chair as far back as he could, placing the blanket on top of him and the pillow behind his head. "I was worried about the six-hour round trip train ride to Eschaton taking up our entire day, but I think you won't be hearing a peep out of me now. I'll tell you one thing; Ali made a mistake not picking the guard shift."

"Well, I guess we still don't know what we're supposed to do yet, so that might change." Noah said, turning to look down the aisle. He didn't see anyone else and assumed the other passengers had boarded different cars on the train.

"At this point, I don't care what it is we have to do." Jake stated, his voice very relaxed from the reclined position. "This is worth it."

Noah laughed. "Yeah. I *am* kind of surprised you're not missing home or anything, though."

"What do you mean?" Jake asked.

"Well, I mean, I'm the one that doesn't really like being at home." Noah explained. "So being away is totally fine for me. I just know how much you like being around your family and stuff. I figured you would miss it."

Jake slipped on the eye mask, pulled the blanket higher up on him, and crossed his arms over his chest like a mummy. "I do love being home." He said. "But that doesn't mean I can't enjoy myself if I'm not there. This is like a vacation. I know I'm not here forever, so I'm just gonna soak it up while I can. And when I get home, I'll be happy to be there, too."

"That's nice." Noah understood where his friend was coming from. "I wish I could have the same mentality."

"Eh, don't worry about being like me." Jake replied, slowly drifting off as the train began to glide down the tracks. The conversation was the only thing keeping him from falling fast asleep. "Everyone has their beasts they have to face. I'm just lucky in this one regard because I don't have to worry about where I want to be. You *will* have to worry about that and figure it out, but that battle will end up affording you some advantages I'll probably never have."

"How so?" Noah wondered. "It just sounds like I have more work to do."

"It's only work if you see it that way." Jake responded. "Think of it as an adventure into the unknown. It's scary and exciting and full of potential."

"It definitely is scary." Noah agreed, reclining his seat back a bit. "How do you think I should start to figure it out?"

"No need to bother asking me." Jake sleepily delivered. "I've never had to face that problem, so I don't know how to solve it, either. It's probably something you'll just have to do yourself."

Noah, despite feeling alone on his journey of self-discovery, actually felt some positive emotions around the autonomy – like it was *his* battle, *his* responsibility, and nobody else had a say in what was right for him. The independence made him feel at peace.

"As for my beasts." Jake continued. "If I'm sticking around Orwell, finding a job that doesn't give me black lung and that still pays well is going to be dang near *impossible*. So there's that. Also I reckon all of you all are gonna up and leave me eventually. That's going to be hard." His speech turned into a mumble as he drifted in and out of consciousness. "But I'm sure it'll be..."

Noah noticed Jake's sentence was cut short, so he turned to look at his friend, who was now completely passed out with his mouth hanging slightly open. Noah laughed at the scene, especially since Jake was donning the sleep mask and had basically converted his seat into a bed. After a second, Noah turned back to his station and began to play with the screen on the seat in front of him, searching for a TV show to watch for the rest of the ride. When he found one, he leaned back and enjoyed the quiet comfort of the insanely luxurious train.

· · · · ●· ● · · · ·

"You boys ready for your first day?" A friendly masculine voice loudly spoke from behind them. Jake was scared into an upright position.

"Geez Louise, man." Jake said, removing his blindfold.

"Sorry, didn't mean to startle ya." The man defended. "But we're here."

"What do you mean?" Jake asked. "Did I sleep the whole way?" He looked out the window and only saw fog.

"Couldn't have slept long." The man said. "Train ride was only 30 minutes."

"There's no way." Jake argued. "Eschaton is not even *remotely* close to Huxley. It's like a three-hour trip one way!"

"I remember my first bullet train." The man joked to the boys behind him, who got a good laugh out of it. "Come on, we gotta go." The man held out a hand to help Jake out of his seat. "I'm Captain Balázs."

"Jake Workman." The still-dazed boy replied, using Captain Balázs' hand to help himself stand up.

"I'm Noah Guthrie." Noah stated, receiving a handshake from the captain. "I've been meaning to ask you, what exactly are we doing today?"

"Let's get this aisle unclogged and I'll tell you on the platform." Balász said, gesturing for the boys to walk in front of him.

"Oh, right." Noah replied, taking the lead. Jake followed him.

When they stepped off the train and onto the platform, Captain Balázs had all the boys gather around for a quick info session.

"Alright, everyone, here's the scoop." Balázs spoke to the group. "Before we go inside The Bistro, let's talk a little bit about what's going on with Eschaton. Many of you probably already know some of this but listen up anyway."

The boys looked behind the speaker and noticed that the station had long windows of dark-tinted glass that stretched about thirty feet in width. They couldn't see inside at all. The only thing that was visible was a red neon sign above the tinted glass door that said 'The Bistro' in cursive.

"Normally, Huxley does not conduct volunteer missions to other cities." Balázs continued. "But for the past few weeks, there have been rumors of some animal or creature that keeps coming around this town and scaring its citizens. Now, you might be wondering why this is of any concern to the city of Huxley, and you would be right to ask that – we all did. But this mission is a direct request from the founder of Huxley herself, so we're going to keep an eye on this city and take care of this problem as a courtesy to her."

The two boys' eyes lit up. Nimkii wanting information about a creature roaming around in West Virginia?! Their interest piqued heavily. Jake raised his hand, catching the attention of the captain, who smiled at the school-like behavior. "Yessir?" He said to Jake.

"Um." Jake looked around. "Is the creature she's looking for the Moth-man?"

"What?" Captain Balázs asked. "No, no, no. Nothing like that. Some re-ports say it's a bear, some say it's a person. We're not entirely sure. But, in case this is your next question, let me go ahead and say no – it is *not* a bear-man."

Everyone chuckled at the captain's joke. Jake let out a friendly smile, a little embarrassed.

"There's no need to be that concerned." Balázs continued. "It's probably just some drugged-out person making a bunch of racket. That, or an animal scavenging for food. Either way, I figure Nimkii just wants us to help out Eschaton as a favor to them since they buy our electricity."

The two friends glanced at each other, not fully believing their captain's logic.

"So, anyway." Balázs wrapped up, taking in a breath and standing up straighter. "Let's go talk to the fat cats inside, and then find ourselves this bear-person." He turned to lead everyone toward The Bistro as the men chuckled again at Balázs' dig toward Jake.

The captain held the door open as everyone shuffled in. Jake and Noah were the last to approach the door. Jake stopped and leaned in toward the captain.

"I don't know how you can have a fiery flying lightning creature for a founder and make fun of me for suggesting that Mothman exists." He said quietly with a hint of annoyance.

"Yeah, I'm sorry." Balázs said sympathetically. "Honestly, I just don't want to get anyone worried. We really have no clue what it is. But I doubt it's anything of that caliber."

"Okay." Jake understood. "Thanks for saying that."

"No problem, sport." Captain replied as he guided the boys inside. "Now, let's introduce you all to some of the people of Eschaton."

Upon crossing the threshold into the building, it was immediately clear that they were standing in a fancy restaurant. The place was almost a cliché – dimly lit, with white tablecloths and candle centerpieces. The walls were a dark red, wine color. On the right-hand wall was a long wooden bar, and there were large paintings on the walls that were also dimly lit by their own little lights hanging above them. The restaurant was packed. Every table was full. The men were wearing either full three-piece suits or tuxedos, and the women were donning sequined gowns and dresses.

"Did we just walk into a breakfast charity auction?" Jake joked toward Noah, who let out a snorty chuckle.

"I mean, it's 10 a.m. on a Tuesday." Jake continued, poking fun at their formality. "Why are they not at work? They're eating club sandwiches with potato chips in nightgowns. I think we can at least save the formal attire for tonight's tuna tartare." The boys started giggling a little too loud and the Captain cleared his throat in a way that told them to stop.

"Captain Balázs, always a pleasure to see you." One of the fat cats with a pot belly said as he walked up to them. He had on a dozen large golden rings and spoke with a slight Italian accent. "I see the guard recruiting efforts have increased since your last visit. Please, introduce me to our two new guests."

"Yes, Mr. Russo," Captain Balázs confirmed. "This, here, is Jake Workman, and this is Noah Guthrie."

"Boys, how do you do?" Russo said as he reached his hand to his heart and took a bow. "My name is Leonardo Russo. Where are you from? Would you like a drink?"

"Uh, sure, sir." Jake replied. "We're from Orwell."

"Oh...very good, then. Very good." Russo returned, looking up to address the rest of the guards. "Please, everyone, you know what to do. Make yourself at home. I will take these boys to find some drinks." Boys, follow me." He turned and began walking toward the bar. The boys followed in suit.

"Linda, Linda, dear," Russo called out as he approached the bar. "Meet the new guard boys".

Linda was in a gown and sitting on one of the bar stools, facing the mirrored wall lined with booze. She had a faux fur garment on her shoulder. "Jake Workman and Noah Guthrie. They're from Orwell. You know where that is." He turned back to them. "Boys, order what you wish. It's on me."

"Oh my..." The woman said, slightly aghast. "Orwell? Surely you must be happy to be out of there and in a more cultured place!"

"You mean here, ma'am?" Jake asked, with a hint of sarcasm.

"Oh, well, I mean anywhere else honestly." She said with a forced laugh, looking to the people around her for approval. They showed some half-smiles in order to appease her.

"I mean, I know we don't have all the fancy stuff Huxley has," Jake said, "but we get by alright."

"Sure you do, dear." The woman said with a weak grin, blankly looking into the mirror as she took a sip of her mojito.

The bartender placed two ice waters on the bar for the boys and asked if he could get them anything else, but they declined.

"So, what do you think of our bistro?" Linda asked. "Isn't it lovely?"

"Uh, yes ma'am. It's a nice place." Noah answered. "Can I ask who made all these paintings on the walls? I've always liked learning about art since I was a kid, but I don't recognize the artist. Well, I assume it's the same artist. They all look like a similar style."

"Oh but don't you just find each one of them so unique?!" Linda said enthusiastically. "I'm surprised you don't recognize the artist! She's very good."

Noah sat there, a bit bewildered, wondering if she was going to answer the question.

"Adelaide Summers is the artist." Russo told the boys. "She's quite good, isn't she, dear?"

"I just love her!" Linda said a little too loud. "Her artwork is everywhere in Eschaton. We really pride ourselves with the amount of wonderful artists we have."

"Well maybe I've heard of some others." Noah said, taking a sip of his water. "Who else is from here?"

"Oh, Leo, what are some of their names?" Linda asked in a dramatic tone, engaging in a heavy eye contact memory recall staring contest with Mr. Russo, tapping her hand on the bar as some kind of ritual to summon the answer. "There's the Summers girl...who else?"

Noah thought it was odd that she was proud of the city's artists and couldn't name more than one off-the-cuff, if that.

"Well, for painters, that's about all we have," Russo answered, "but there's a great woodworker boy named, um, Ted Gillispie, I think. He's made a couple of beautiful wooden items for some of our residents."

"That's cool…" Noah said, not sure if he wanted to pursue clarity around the vague term 'wooden items' with people who appeared to not know that much about the subject. "Do you have an art gallery around here? I hear Eschaton is a big town."

"Some would call it a city, wouldn't they?" Leo snootily joked to Linda, who laughed with him. "We had an art gallery awhile back…but now it's something else, isn't it, Linda?"

"Yes, yes, yes." She said. "It closed down two or three years ago. Then it was a country restaurant after that, then a milkshake place, then a boutique, then a thrift shop, and now I think it's for lease again!"

Noah was a little startled at the high turnover rate. That was a lot of businesses to open and close in a matter of a few years.

"Oh!" Russo said, giving the bar a slap as if an idea struck him. He looked at Noah. "That just gave me a great idea – one that I think you'd be particularly interested in, young man." He leaned against the bar to explain himself.

"How old are you?" He asked Noah, trying to figure out if his idea had legs.

"Um, I'm 14, sir." Noah answered cautiously.

"Hmmm…" Russo contemplated.

"What's your idea?" Noah asked, mostly so Russo could get on with his point.

"Well, I was just trying to figure out, since the legal working age is 16 here, if there would be any way to let you start your own art gallery."

"You mean you want me to start an art gallery…here?"

"Yes! I think it would be great." Russo kept thinking. "We could probably work with the city council to get you a permit."

"This is my first time in Eschaton, sir. And I've never even thought about starting an art gallery. I was just wondering if you all had one because…"

"Ah, not to worry, boy!" Russo interrupted. "If there's a will, there's a way. I think you should save up for a couple years and then move here. It'll be great! Surely better than anything you could wish for back in Orwell, yes?"

Jake grew furious at Russo's odd and sudden planning of Noah's life as well as his disses toward their hometown.

"Maybe it's something I'll need to think on." Noah said, just hoping to move on from whatever aggressive proposal was happening.

"Well, you think on it for a bit." Russo insisted. "But I think it's a great idea! Don't you, Linda?"

Linda slammed the rest of her early-morning mojito, raising it in the air. "Absolutely, darling. Terrific idea."

Russo gave a nod to Linda for her commendation. "You'll have to watch out, though." He continued. "The man who leases out that building is a friend of mine, but he's also Linda's ex-husband!" The fat cat burst out in laughter.

"I'm glad you kept him!" Linda joked again, letting out a forced cackle to meet Leo's laughter. The boys hadn't so much as giggled at a single joke from any of these people since they walked up to the bar. It's almost like they weren't even telling jokes – just saying crude or uncomfortable phrases and forcing laughter through them. It was an extremely unpleasant and unnatural experience.

"Time's up boys." Captain Balázs said from a distance as he approached the bar. "Ready to stop socializing and start working?"

A wave of relief washed over them. "Yes, yes we are." Jake said strongly, taking a sip of his water, slamming it down, and hopping off the bar stool. Noah gave a slight grin and an insincere goodbye to Linda, while Jake outright ignored her completely. They didn't really care for her and her oddly judgmental, vanity-driven conversation style. Russo followed the group of guards to the opposite end of the restaurant from where they entered, where another door stood closed. They opened it and shuffled into a large vestibule-like area, surrounded on both sides by tinted glass windows. It was clear the next door would lead them outside into the city. Captain Balázs raised his hands to get everyone's attention.

"Alright, now like I said," he spoke in a loud volume so the group could hear him, "we aren't really that concerned with what's out there, but we also don't want you all being at risk in case something goes south. So, first, it's important for you all to be aware that a low hum has been reported to take place whenever the person or creature is nearby. Which means you'll need to keep an ear out and alert the others if you hear it. And second, I can't in good conscience send you out there undefended, especially since we don't know what we're dealing with, so head on down to the metal cabinets sitting against the back wall and we'll hook you up with some protective equipment. We probably won't need it, but it's just a precaution."

The group began walking toward the cabinets at the other end of the room.

"Think he has any protection against Linda?" Noah joked quietly to Jake, who let out a burst of laughter air.

"Or against uncomfortable conversations about opening an art gallery at the age of 16?" Jake fired back.

"In a strange place?"

"When literally every business that has tried to go in there has failed?"

"Including an art gallery!" Noah laughed out of disbelief, then noticed the rest of the guards were walking past them with knives, baseball bats, and even a few guns.

"What the heck?" Noah rhetorically said to Jake as they approached Captain Balázs, who was handing out the equipment.

"Alright, boys." the captain said, turning to search the inventory for something that would work for them. "You all are much too young for guns, so that's out of the question. Knives too, I think." He kept rummaging around. "Ah! Here we go."

When Balázs turned to face them, he was holding a taser gun and a net.

"Jake, you can have this taser." He handed Jake the taser gun. "It's pretty simple, just point and shoot. It only has one charge, though, so don't waste it. The safety is currently activated on the left side of the gun, so you'll want to flip that off before you shoot. That'll help protect you in case an animal gets too close to you and you need to subdue it."

"Um, okay." Jake said, confused and looking at the weapon.

"And Noah, the best I can do for you is this net." He admitted. "Now, I know it might not look like much, but I bet you all can work together if something happens, you know? Like, tase the animal and wrap it up in the net. You all can come up with something. I'm sure of it." The captain was doing his best to convince the boys that the taser-net combo was a solid option, but his effort was not succeeding.

"Yeah, I guess we'll just hope we're not the ones who have to take care of the animal, or whatever it is." Noah said, pointing to how stupid a taser-net combo sounded.

"Yeah...I guess so." The captain agreed. "Anyway!" He yelled to the group. "Let's get out there and make Nimkii proud."

Everyone followed Captain Balázs outside. Noah and Jake were, once again, in the tail-end of the group. As they were shuffling out the door, Mr. Russo fell back and made eye contact with Noah, who let out a sigh, knowing his conversation with the fat cat was not over.

"Mr. Guthrie." Russo snuck in. "I really am excited to show you that leasing opportunity. It would be such a perfect addition to our city! Trust me on that. Do you want to have a family one day?"

"I honestly don't know." Noah replied.

"Well, that's okay!" Russo sidestepped. "Surely, you'll want to have a family one of these days. Especially if you're a hard-working gallery owner. And there really isn't a better place to live than Eschaton when it comes to family values. We have a *strong* community and really see to it that our children are taken care of."

"Well, I guess we'll have to see." Noah said, trying to end the conversation.

"Yeah." Russo began picking up on Noah's distaste for the idea. "Maybe so."

The boys were finally able to take their attention away from Mr. Russo and focus on the outdoor space in Eschaton's city center. The first thing they noticed was a small white church in the middle of the city, completely surrounded by taller stone and brick buildings that towered over it. The steeple on the church was broken but was still hanging on by one board. The buildings were broken too, with shattered glass and what looked like years-worth of winter muck on their facades. Many of the buildings were boarded up and looked like they had been abandoned or closed down for some time. The place felt like a ghost town. The only cars that weren't clearly left to rust were sitting in the parking lot that the group was traveling through outside of The Bistro.

"Don't mind the cars." Leo told the group, walking ahead of them. "The Bistro is in a very popular part of the city."

"It looks like it's in the only part of the city." Jake joked quietly to Noah. Captain Balázs heard the comment and whacked him on the back of the head.

As they made their way past the parking lot and toward the church, Mr. Russo turned around and started backpedaling like a tour guide.

"I want to show you folks some things we in Eschaton have done to provide for the community." He began to point out what he was referring to. "Take a look at these amenities the church has created for our children. There's this nice playground over here that the kids like to play on, and there's a little dog park over there."

Noah and Jake looked and saw the playground, which sported one tire swing with a regular swing set next to it. The regular swing set had two normal swings and one baby swing. The chains looked rusted, even from a distance, and the paint was about half-chipped off. They looked around but couldn't find the dog park Mr. Russo was talking about, unless he was referring to the little patch of mud next to the playground, barely the size of the average front yard in Orwell.

"And of course we have our beloved Eschatonian church here," Mr. Russo said, looking toward Jake and Noah, "which is what you two will be protecting while the other more experienced guards hunt for the creature."

The boys looked at their Captain. "Is that right?" Noah asked.

"Yeah, Mr. Russo is right, there." Balázs admitted. "It'll be safer for you two to stay here."

"But...what if you need a net?" Noah fired the question at Balázs, who closed his eyes and forced a slight, defeated frown upon hearing the remark.

"I think the net may be best utilized here at the church." The captain answered, diplomatically. "But here's a walkie talkie in case you need to get in contact with us." He handed Jake the device.

"Okay, thanks." Jake addressed the captain. "But I'm still confused. Why does this church need guarded?"

"Some of the reports have said that the person or animal we're looking for keeps trying to break into the church." Balázs explained. "We're not entirely sure why. But, just in case the subject in question gets any bright ideas to try something while we're on the hunt for it, we want to make sure we have all of our bases covered by guarding the church, too."

"I guess that makes sense." Jake said, a little disappointed, feeling like he was going to miss out on the hunt and discovering firsthand what creature this was.

"This church is very sacred and special to our town." Mr. Russo added. "You boys have an immensely important job, making sure it's not attacked."

"Is that what happened to the steeple?" Noah asked.

"What do you mean?" Russo returned.

"Well, the steeple is barely hanging on." Noah pointed out the obvious. "Did the monster attack the church while it was trying to break in?"

"Oh, no." Leo answered. "That happened about two decades ago in a pretty bad windstorm. We just don't have a good carpenter to make a new one."

"W...well...why don't you get that Ted guy to make a new one?" Noah pressed. "He's a woodworker, right?"

"Yeah, he is, but we probably won't hire him for the job." Leo vaguely answered, clearly trying to deflect the topic.

"How come?" Jake asked in place of Noah, now curious as to why the city wouldn't hire their only good woodworker to fix a wooden steeple on a church that they, moments ago, described as 'sacred and special'.

"Well, I guess the people of Eschaton don't enjoy putting our money into artists who aren't a tightknit part of our community." Russo explained.

"Oh, gotcha." Noah said to Russo, picking up on what he was implying. "So he doesn't come around The Bistro much."

"Yes, exactly!" Leo confirmed. "He also doesn't come to church very often, and we'd really prefer to give our money to someone who is more invested in the city's activities, which Ted just isn't. He's normally too busy teaching history at the high school or building things in his shop."

"Sounds like this *Ted* guy is a real jerk." Jake sarcastically whispered to Noah, which caught the attention of Mr. Russo.

"What was that, young sir?" Russo asked, annoyed by their secretive exchange.

"Oh, nothing Mr. Russo." Noah defended. "Jake was just saying that it was a shame the church's steeple broke."

"Well, yes...it is..." Russo tried to be understanding, though he was still suspicious that the boys weren't telling the truth to him. "But one thing at a time, I suppose. Our chief concern right now is this thing that keeps scaring our citizens. Once we get that sorted out, we'll start to worry about things like steeples."

"Mr. Russo is correct." The captain stepped in. "You boys stay here. If we're not back by nightfall, feel free to have dinner at The Bistro. There's attire inside the church that you can change into. And please, try to stay out of trouble, you two. We'll be back before you know it."

The captain, Mr. Russo, and the other guards turned and started walking away from the church.

"Jesus." Jake let out as soon as they were out of earshot. "That was exhausting."

"You're telling me." Noah remarked. "I think if I were any older Leo would've up and punched me by now."

"You were definitely annoying the bejesus out of him." Jake agreed with a laugh.

Noah shook his head at the thought of what just happened.

"Remember how, on the train, you said that I would have to go out and find a place that I felt comfortable with?" Noah asked his friend.

"Heh, yeah." Jake confirmed.

"I get the weird feeling this isn't it." Noah joked.

Jake let out a little belly chuckle. "Ah, you'll be fine." He said. "I can't guarantee the next place you visit will be the winner, but I know one thing...it surely won't be anything like whatever this is..."

"Gosh, I don't know how it could." Noah replied. "What a bunch of completely out-of-touch people."

"Eh, let 'em live in their dream world." Jake stared out at all the abandoned buildings. "I would probably black out my windows and live in denial if I lived here, too."

Noah released a small burst of breath. "Yeah, I figure I would do the same..."

The two friends took a moment, standing outside the church, and processed their day up to that point. After about a minute, Noah snapped out of it.

"I'm gonna head inside the church, use the restroom, and see if I can find any snacks or something." He said. "I'm starving."

"Yeah, grab me some, too, if you see anything." Jake requested. "But hurry. If this monster-person attacks the church, I'll need my trusty taser-net combo buddy to help me subdue it."

Noah gave a strong salute to his pal and walked inside the church.

CHAPTER SIX

THE SECRET AT ESCHATON

Inside the church, it was mostly what Noah expected – wooden pews facing a slightly raised stage, white walls all around – but there were some exceptions. The first of the exceptions were the two huge televisions mounted above the stage, flanked by stacked speakers that stretched from the floor to the ceiling. The scene looked like a concert venue – more of a place for entertainment than for worship – and Noah felt like all the technology sucked the sacredness out of the space.

He walked over to the stereo system and began rummaging around the CDs. Most of the titles were at least two decades old – some three – and a majority of their covers had faded in color. He placed the CDs back on the table and looked up to inspect the vaulted ceiling, which was an old, stale white color and had a water-damaged spot near the eave. He found himself completely disappointed at the sight. It felt like no love was put into the space at all. He couldn't help but think about how all the artists who designed the European cathedrals' mosaics, paintings, and sculptures would find this room completely uninspiring.

Noah was enjoying his ever-increasing thoughts of judgment, but a higher calling began speaking to him – his bladder – so he exited the nave in search of a restroom.

After he was finished with his business, Noah snooped around the rest of the church in search of some snacks. The first room he picked, sort of a medium-sized room lined with foldable tables, had a kitchenette attached to it. Despite the general expectation that a kitchenette would hold some snacks, he came up mostly short, aside from a couple of two liters in the fridge. Noah figured the church people kept the snacks locked away for the exact reason he was in there, so he decided to continue his search elsewhere.

Noah's next target was the pastor's office. As he made his way down the hall to look for it, he noticed a low hum coming from behind a door marked 'For Church Elders Only'. He figured it was an old HVAC unit, or something mechanical like that. He tried to open the door out of curiosity and found that it was locked, so he kept walking down the hall. Eventually he came to a door marked 'Pastor's Office,' but that door was locked, too. He got annoyed and felt around the door frame, searching for a key, and was surprised when he found one resting on the top part of the frame. He grabbed it and unlocked the door.

The pastor's office was kind of a wreck. Books thrown about on the floor, broken boxes toppling over with supplies, and a bunch of general items just thrown all over the place. Noah checked the boxes and found one that had bags of orange cheese crackers in it – a score for him – then he found another filled to the brim with little bags of gummies – a major nab for Jake. He grabbed as much as his pockets could hold, since his hands would be holding the two liters, and ran out of the room to show off his loot.

As Noah sped out of the room, he collided with Jake, who was briskly jogging down the hallway to find his friend. One of the two liters busted upon their impact, and the other busted on the ground when Noah dropped it out of shock from the first one exploding, covering them both in a carbonated mess.

"Dude!" Noah said, wiping soda off his shirt. "What are you doing? You scared the crap outta me."

Jake's eyes were wide and panicky. He was out of breath and didn't say anything.

"Brother, are you okay?" Noah asked.

"No." Jake forced out from his rapid breathing. "Bear."

"Bear?"

"Bear."

"What? Here?"

"Outside."

"Oh. Why are you out of breath?"

Jake shot a glare at Noah, who wasn't understanding the urgency of the situation.

"The bear ran towards me."

"Well, did you provoke it?"

"Noah, Jesus!" Jake let out an annoyed eye roll. His breath was returning. "I didn't provoke the freaking bear. We gotta skedaddle, dude. It's coming here."

The hum from the Church Elder's door grew louder. The boys began speaking louder to compensate for it, though they weren't consciously aware of it.

"Jake, we're inside the church. We're fine. Did you lock the door?"

"I mean, yeah…but it's a bear, dude. That won't make a difference."

"I'm sure it forgot all about you the second you walked inside."

"I don't know…it had a crazy look in its eye."

Noah laughed at his friend's goofiness. "Come on, man, I got some snacks for you. I had soda as well, but you see what happened there…let's grab some paper towels in the kitchen over here."

They began walking down the hall and toward the kitchenette that was attached to the room next to the nave. Jake kept checking behind them to make sure the beast wasn't lurking around.

Noah ripped the paper towel roll off its holder and tossed it to Jake. "Let's clean this up and listen to some of these old gospel CDs while we eat."

They began walking down the hall to where the spilled drinks were. The hum was now so loud that it was vibrating the Church Elder's door. Noah yelled over the commotion.

"I think they've got an HVAC unit out of whack in there…or a generator or something. It's been doing that the whole time I've been in here, but it keeps getting worse."

Jake looked over and observed the metal handle shaking back and forth. He imagined briefly that something inside was trying to fight its way out of the door, but that thought scared him, so he snapped back to the task at hand.

Jake bent down and began laying strips of paper towels over the soda and watched as the liquid spread throughout the material. After he laid down the third strip of paper, a loud thud sounded from the other end of the hall. He and Noah looked at each other.

"You think Captain Balazs is back so soon?" Noah asked, beginning to hurriedly walk toward the front door.

"STOP!" Jake shouted. Noah stopped in his tracks and turned around. "What's wrong?"

Another thud sounded at the door.

Jake's eyes were wide and panicky again. He mouthed, "It's. The. Bear."

Noah looked down the hall slowly, then back at Noah, realizing Jake's assumption was not a total impossibility after all. He scrambled over to Jake and moved them into the pastor's room so they could talk quietly out of the hallway.

"Why would a bear want to get in the church?" Noah asked.

"I don't know, dude. I mean, for one, I think it hates me. But didn't the captain also say that the bear has been here before?"

"Oh shoot, you're right...he did. Shoot shoot shoot. Okay. We gotta think. How do we get outta here?"

"Is there a back door?"

"No." Noah replied. "The temple in the back is all walls."

Jake looked toward the window in the pastor's room. "Let's climb out the window. If we're quiet, I bet we can sneak away and call for help."

"Good idea." Noah said.

They rushed over to the window, which was certainly the building's original by the looks of it. It had a latch that unlocked the bottom half of the window, allowing it to slide up.

Noah squeezed the latch as hard as he could, but the thing wouldn't budge.

A thud came once again from the front door, followed by two more in rapid succession.

"Crap man, it really wants in here." Jake said. "Here, let me try."

He applied as much torque to the latch as his hands could muster, but he, too, gave up out of the pain that began growing in his hands.

"This darn latch has been painted shut over and over again for like at least fifty coats."

"It looks like the whole window has." Noah surrendered. "We need a new plan."

He and Jake stood there for a moment in hurried contemplation, figuring the bear was going to break in at any moment.

After about ten seconds, Jake had an idea.

"Hey, man, didn't Balázs say that people kept hearing a hum whenever the creature would come around."

"Yeah...why do you say that?" Noah looked blankly at Jake for a split second before his brain caught up to the point faster than it took Jake to begin replying. "Oh, oh! The HVAC unit!"

"I ain't got any better guesses."

"Me neither. Let's see if we can turn it off. It might save our hides."

They began walking quickly into the hallway and toward the door. Noah stopped.

"Oh, shoot!"

"What?"

"It's locked. We need a key." Noah ran over to the frame around the Elder's door and felt around. "This is how I got into the pastor's office." His search came up empty.

"Crap, man, this is bad."

The next thud that struck the door was accompanied by the sound of cracking wood and a loud roar.

"Okay, okay, okay. It's definitely the bear. You try to kick down the door. I'm going to look for a key."

"You got it." Jake replied, as he stomped into the area of the door next to the handle. The vibrations from the impact hurt his foot. He certainly didn't have the proper footwear for door kicking, but he continued anyway.

Noah rummaged around the pastor's office. He looked in drawers, on bookshelves, and even crawled under the desk trying to find a spare key, but he came up empty-handed. Then he noticed a little box sitting on the pastor's table. It was metal and had a lock, but when Noah tried to open it, the lid opened with no problem. Noah looked inside and found about fifteen keys that had no labels or tags.

He ran back into the hall and saw Jake hurdling his body into the door and bouncing right off. Jake gave up at the sight of Noah's reappearance and leaned against the wall, out of breath.

"I can't do it, man. I don't know how to break down a door. I'm no bear."

As he said that, the front doors sounded like they were blasted open, followed by the sound of metal crashing onto the tiled floor.

"Ah *frick man*, he's *here*." Jake moaned.

Noah ran over to the door with the box of keys and began trying them one by one. The door was vibrating so hard that Noah was having trouble fitting the keys in the lock. Some he even dropped onto the ground accidentally and immediately gave up on, hoping those weren't the winners.

"Noah." Jake said.

"Not now."

"...Noah."

"What?"

Jake didn't respond.

Noah looked behind him to check on his friend, who was frozen in a stare down the hallway, fear washing over his whole body. Noah looked in the same direction and saw a massive black bear at the end of the hall, staring directly at them, with a mean-looking expression on its face.

"Noah...it hates us." Jake said fearfully under his breath.

Noah went back to his keys. He tried another one with no success. Then another. Finally, one key turned the lock.

"Jake, I've got it." Noah said, but his friend was completely lost in eye contact with the bear, which had been slowly approaching them as Noah was trying out the keys.

Noah looked over at the bear and it stopped walking toward them. He felt in that moment that the black bear might actually be afraid of him. He remembered how in school they taught him the 'If it's brown, lay down. If it's black, fight back' rule. This thought gave him an idea.

Noah turned to squarely face the black bear. He flexed his skinny arms, made them as wide as possible to look larger, and let out the best roar any eighth-grade boy could attempt – which meant that it was weak, not scary at all, and cracked at the peak of intensity.

The bear looked confused for a moment, then returned to anger, letting out a roar that sent chills down Noah's legs.

"Okay, bad idea." Noah said as he grabbed a still-petrified Jake by his shirt and dragged him through the Church Elder's door, pulling them both into a pitch-black room. Noah slammed the door behind them and made sure to lock it. A wave of temporary relief washed over him, knowing there was another barrier between them and the creature. He closed his eyes and took a second to gather himself.

The boys' hearts were beating so heavily in their chests that they both felt they could faint at any moment. Jake remembered dismissing every red flag that led them to this point and thought about how much he regretted it. He thought about Ali, and how she must be having such a better time than they were right now. He hoped they would live long enough to see her again.

The hum was now at a deafening volume. The boys stood completely still as they watched the shadow of the bear cross in front of the crack of light coming from the bottom of the door. They could hear it grunting on the other side.

"We have to find a light switch." Jake yelled over the hum into the darkness, unsure of his friend's exact location.

The bear slammed into the door, scaring Jake so much that he screamed.

"Come on, man, feel around!" Jake begged.

They used their hands to feel along the dark walls of the room in search of a light switch. It took a few seconds, but Noah finally found one. He flicked it on, and a distant dim lightbulb lit up from the bottom of a concrete staircase next to them, clearly leading into some kind of basement.

"Oh, *heck* no, dude...you've gotta be kidding me!" Jake loudly complained.

"What? You wanna go back out there with the bear?" Noah shouted at Jake, who immediately understood that this was their only option. "First, let's turn this hum off. Then we'll call for help."

"If we don't get murdered first." Jake returned.

"Right!" Noah confirmed.

Noah led the cautious descent into the creepy basement, with Jake following closely behind him.

Everything down there was covered in dust – the floor, the knickknacks laying on the ground, and the storage shelves, not to mention the abundance of cobwebs and dead insects lying about. Many items couldn't even be recognized because there was so much dust obscuring their surfaces. The faint light from the bulb, attached to a chain overhead, made the small space feel even smaller – and that much creepier. As the boys looked around; it was clear that there was no HVAC unit in sight, which meant they had no clue where the hum was coming from.

Noah tried to yell over the overwhelmingly voluminous drone to Jake, but it was so loud at this point that Jake couldn't hear him, so he grabbed Jake's shoulder to get his attention. Jake mouthed "What?"

"We need to find the source." Noah mouthed and gestured.

"The sword?" Jake asked, holding an imaginary hilt up to Noah in confusion to show what he meant.

"No, the noise!" Noah yelled as loud as he could, pointing at his ears. Luckily, Jake understood what Noah was gesturing and returned an 'Oh!' reaction with a thumbs up to indicate he had received the message.

At this disorienting sound level in the echo-heavy basement, it was impossible to perceive the sound's direction. The boys began dusting off each object, hoping to figure it out by process of elimination. They peeled back cobwebs that had been abandoned by their creators for years. Jake picked up a dusty doll off the ground, and a bunch of beetles scattered in all directions from where it had lied.

Noah began inspecting items on the storage shelves one by one. Nothing seemed to make sense. There was a vase that caught his attention on the top shelf, but it was out of his reach, so he looked around for something to give him a lift to get up there. Noah eliminated his options one by one, until he noticed a dusty wooden chest sitting in a corner next to the shelves. It had large iron rings on its sides, so he reached down to grab one and pull the chest in front of the shelves.

As his hand made contact with the cold iron handle, the vibrations emanating from it squeezed every muscle in his arm. He pulled away in shock and kicked the chest in a fear-based reaction as if something had bitten him. When he did, the hum immediately stopped, but the boys' ears kept ringing as they readjusted to the volume change.

The sound of Captain Balázs' voice came from the walkie talkie in Jake's pocket, which Jake had completely forgotten about in the adrenaline rush.

"Mr. Workman, do you copy?" It said. "Mr. Workman."

Jake's ears were still ringing, but he scrambled to get the device. He fumbled it around until his fingers found the 'talk' button.

"Yes, Captain, I'm here." He said in a slightly panicked voice.

"You all alright over there?" Balázs asked. "You weren't responding."

"No sir. We're being hunted by a bear. It broke into the church."

"Are you serious? Are either of you hurt?"

"Yes, I'm serious! But no, we're not hurt...yet. You gotta get down here quick. It could find us at any second."

"Ah, crap." Balázs exhaled. "Boys, we gotta go!" He yelled to the other guards. "Jake, we'll be there in ten minutes. Find a place to hide."

"Already covered, sir. Please hurry."

No response came from the device.

"Okay." Jake looked up to talk to Noah. "We'll just have to hold up here for a few minutes until our backup arrives. Hopefully the bear will calm down and stop pursuing us now that the noise is gone."

"Yeah, let's hope." Noah nodded his head in understanding. "God..." He flicked his hand, which still felt the effects of the stun. "Why the heck was that box vibrating so heavily?" He kicked it again out of anger.

"What's in it?" Jake asked.

"I don't know." Noah answered, looking down at it. "I'm a little curious, though. It's got a big metal lock on it. And I didn't see any keys on the shelf."

"Don't worry, I think I saw a spare key over here." Jake noted as he turned around and went to the other side of the room.

"A spare key?" Noah wondered.

When Jake returned, he was holding a large crowbar. He walked up to the chest, shoved it under the lid, and slammed his foot down on the bar, cracking the box open.

"Huh. Well done." Noah said to him, turning back to the chest.

They both leaned over the open container and strained to see in the low light what was inside.

"You reach in." Jake suggested.

"Are you kidding me?" Noah questioned. "You reach in! I've already had my hand shocked once by it."

"Please help me." A voice spoke from inside the chest. The boys, with a slight delay in recognizing the third party, fell back in fear of the voice. Noah tried to grab on to the storage shelves for balance, and his instability shifted the entire shelf, sending the vase, once resting on top of it, crashing onto the concrete floor below. Jake, who was turned around and trying to find cover, was so scared by the crash that he began running back upstairs for safety, and when he reached the top of the stairs, the bear let out another roar, scaring him halfway back down the staircase.

"What the heck is going on?!" Jake yelled from the railing.

Noah gathered himself and stood back up, sliding broken pieces of glass to the side as he crept up to the chest.

"Who's in there?" Noah asked the box.

"My name is Kanati." The voice answered.

Jake's eyes opened wide as he made the connection as to what was going on and began racing down the stairs. "What?!" He shouted during his descent.

"Please." The unseen Kanati spoke from inside the box. "The bear is here to help me. Can you bring me to it?"

Jake ran up to the container. "Kanati. Hi, I'm Jake. Noah is here with me. We, um, know Ani."

"You do?" Kanati asked. "Please, get me out of here. Before those men come back. They keep trying to trap and kill the animals I'm calling to free me."

In that moment, everything clicked for the two boys. They understood Nimkii's motivation for sending a search party through Eschaton – she suspected that her father was still alive. How else could one explain the low-toned hum and the appearance of such large animals in a populated area? Forest creatures wouldn't normally just do that naturally.

"Here." Jake spoke to the box. "Let's get you out of there."

"Please, I warn you." Kanati cautioned the boys. "I am not a pleasant sight to witness."

"That's okay." Jake responded without thinking as he reached into the dark space and pulled out a human-like head. "Oh my God!" He yelled in fear, dropping the head onto the floor below, then feeling an instant rush of guilt. "I'm so sorry, I'm so sorry." He hurriedly and uncomfortably picked it back up. "I completely forgot you would be like this."

"It's okay." Kanati tried to calm him. "I would have had the same reaction, I'm sure."

"Can I...put you back in the chest?" Jake asked, holding the head far away from him, trying to not make eye contact with it.

"That will be okay for now." Kanati agreed.

"Oh geez, thank you so much."

Jake carefully placed the nature god's head back into the chest, and as he let go, he shuffled backwards in an attempt to get away from it, brushing his hands against the sides of his pants.

"Kanati?" He asked carefully toward the box.

"Yes?" The god responded.

"I want to help you out, but there are guys coming here, looking for this bear, who will be here any minute. If we give you to the bear now, they'll catch both of you."

Kanati let out a sigh. "You're right." He said, disheartened.

"It's okay though. We'll just have to keep you down here and come back for you."

"No! If they have any suspicion that you've found me down here, they'll move me somewhere else, and you won't ever find me again."

"Shoot, he's right." Noah looked at Jake, who stood in contemplation, staring at the box, looking for a solution.

"So...hmm." Jake rested his chin on his thumb, buried in thought. "Give me a second to figure this out." Another brief moment passed. "The bear upstairs is here for you...so...does that mean you're controlling it?"

"Not controlling." Kanati responded. "But I am able to telepathically communicate with it."

"Okay, that's actually sick." Noah let out.

"For real." Jake acknowledged. "But there's no time to get into that. So...how can we use the bear to our advantage here? We need to distract the guards long enough for us to escape."

"Without hurting the bear." Noah added.

Jake, realizing the bear would be in danger if it was still in the church when the men showed up, let out a sigh. "Yeah, the bear thing won't work."

An idea came to Noah. "Wait, Jake, how much time do we have before the guards get here?"

"I don't know." Jake pondered. "Maybe five minutes at best."

"Okay, I think I have an idea." Noah announced. "Kanati, can you tell the bear to get out of here as fast as it can and find somewhere safe to go? So it doesn't get hurt."

"Yes, of course." Kanati agreed. Another hum came from the chest, this time brief, and when it ended, the boys could hear the subfloor bending above their heads as the bear hurried out of the church.

"I'm so sorry, but I can't get over how cool that is." Jake let out.

"Okay, Jake." Noah refocused his friend. "Did you see the sound setup in the temple?"

"Yeah." Jake confirmed.

"Okay, I need you to go there and do me a favor." Noah requested. "I'll take care of the rest."

"Okay." Jake was getting excited to hear Noah's plan.

"We have to find a way to distract the guards long enough to get Kanati out of here." Noah explained. "But Kanati, I'm going to need your help, too."

"Anything you need." Kanati joined in.

"Good." Noah said. "Here's the plan."

• • • • • • • • •

Captain Balázs and the rest of the guards slowly spread out in a formation that covered the entire front of the church.

"Okay men, there's a bear in there with Jake and Noah." He directed them. "That bear has been terrorizing this town for weeks. Subdue it however you can."

The men held on to their bats, tranquilizer guns, swords, and firearms tightly as they gave a confirming nod to their captain.

"LaFon." Balázs called out. "You and I are the only ones with guns. Let's stay ahead of the others for their own safety. When I say 'three', we're going to rush into the church and make sure it's clear. Got it?"

"Yessir." LaFon said, clutching his pistol with two hands as he slowly walked parallel with the captain up to the front doors.

"One." The captain said, taking a moment to look back at his men.

"Two."

The men's hearts were beating heavily from the anticipation of conflict.

"Three!" Balázs yelled, as he and LaFon slammed their feet into the half-opened church doors, bursting them wide open.

"Help!" Jake yelled from the back of the church. "We're in here!"

"Come on, everyone." The captain signaled for his men to rush into the church. "Last one in, find a way to close the door behind us so the thing doesn't get out."

The men rushed into the building, periodically checking behind them as they brisked through the hallway. Some tested the doors along the way, but each one was closed and locked.

The guards funneled into the windowless temple in the back of the church, and just as the last one stepped through the threshold, every light in the church shut off and plummeted the room into darkness. The men began to yell to their captain, looking for direction, but before he could give it to them, the gigantic stack of speakers on the stage began to play "I Wish We'd All Been Ready" at full volume. The loud guitar pierced their ears as the voices in the recordings deafened them with warnings of the rapture.

Nobody in the temple could hear a word anyone else was saying. The men who were listening to the lyrics felt a sense of eeriness pass over them. Some tried to feel around the walls to gain a sense of where they were, while others just yelled, hoping someone outside would hear them. What they didn't think of was that anyone who *could* hear them was well within the walls of The Bistro, lost in their own luxurious microcosm.

Meanwhile, Noah and Jake, in full tuxedos – mostly for the sake of looking cool, but also because their original clothes were covered in soda – pulled themselves out of the broken-off section of the steeple on the second floor and walked onto the roof.

"Kanati, now!" Jake yelled down toward the bag he was carrying.

Two black Nokota horses appeared from behind the church, stopping just under the church's eaves.

With the net tied-off to one of the steeple's posts, they lowered themselves off the roof and onto the horses.

"Alright, Noah, you good?" Jake asked his friend, who was getting situated on his horse's back.

Noah caught his bearings. "Yessir."

"Alright." Jake said, wrapping the horse's mane around his hand. "Kanati, get us out of here."

Kanati let out another hum, and the horses took off, carrying the tuxedoed boys on their backs, charging out of Eschaton and into the forest. They broke into the tree line and ran parallel to the train tracks, headed for Huxley. Noah looked to his right and saw the black bear, sitting deep in the forest, completely unharmed, scratching its back on a tree in the distance. He smiled for a moment at the success of his plan, then refocused on the area in front of him.

· · • • · • • • · ·

Meanwhile, back at the church, the song struck its last chord, giving the men the ability to hear once again – and their captain the ability to coordinate an escape from the dark temple. When the last of the guards made it outside, most of the men were so relieved to be alive and out of the church that they had completely forgotten about why they were there in the first place. Captain Balázs hadn't forgotten, however. The boys were gone, and there was no bear. He knew they were up to something, so he jogged over to The Bistro to tell Leo what had just unfolded.

Moments later, Leo would, in a panic, rush over to the church, make his way into the basement, and discover that Eschaton's best-kept-secret had just been stolen.

"Captain Balázs." He would say. "It appears the boys have stolen something from our church that was of great importance to us."

"What item?" Balázs would reply.

"I cannot say. But I need you to do a full search of the city. Lock down the train. Don't let it go anywhere. They couldn't have gone far."

"Yessir." Balázs would comply. "We will make sure they don't leave the city, sir. And we'll return your item."

What the two men wouldn't know was that Noah and Jake were speeding far out of the reaches of Eschaton on horseback.

· · · · · ● · ● · · · ·

Once they were well out of town, Jake called for the horses to stop.

"What's going on?" Noah asked his friend, who was unfolding his satchel.

"Kanati, I have one more favor to ask." Jake spoke to the godhead in the bag.

"What is your request?"

"Can animals speak to other telepathic beings?"

"Yes, they can."

"Good. I need an animal that can deliver a message for Ani."

"Okay, give me a moment." Kanati said, closing his eyes and releasing another low-toned drone into the forest. Now that they were outside, it was cool to see how the hum's vibrations rattled the leaves on the trees.

Seconds later, a little red cardinal flew over and landed on Noah's shoulder.

"Oh, hey, look!" Noah called to his friend. "He's here!"

"Kanati," Jake directed, "tell the bird to fly southwest. It will find a broken factory in a field next to a small town called Orwell – that's the town where Ani lives. Tell the bird to fly inside the factory and find an all-black monster with red eyes."

"Why are we sending this message to a monster?" Kanati asked. "Why not just tell Ani directly?"

Jake let out an "um...", looking to Noah for help, not sure how to explain to Kanati that his children had been cursed and deformed for what they did to him.

"Ani lives in a place that would be hard for the bird to find." Noah lied. "The monster knows where he is though...and lives close by...so he can give Ani the message."

"If you're sure..." Kanati let it go. "What's the message?"

"The message," Jake continued, "is for Ani to meet us at Huxley, the large domed city to the east, near the Great Bridge. Tell him we are in trouble and will need his help. And for the bird to not be afraid when he sees the monster. It will look scary, but it won't harm him."

"Okay," Kanati said, closing his eyes for a moment. The cardinal flew off of Noah's shoulder and disappeared into the forest, heading southwest. "It is done." Kanati spoke.

"Thank you." Jake kindly said into the bag.

"Alright, let's get back to it." Noah said. "We have a lot of ground to cover, and we'll need to stop for food and sleep along the way."

"Sounds good." Jake replied. "I'm excited to see Ali again."

"Yeah, me too." Noah agreed.

The boys tapped the sides of their shoes on the horses and continued riding toward Huxley, all the while knowing Captain Balázs, the Eschaton Watch Guard, and a furious Leonardo Russo would eventually discover that they had left the town and would come looking for them.

BISTRO

Chapter Seven

Lightning Bugs

As the boys were on horseback, headed toward Huxley, Ali was finishing up her first shift in Huxley's media department. Her day up to that point had been very relaxing, unlike her friends'. She slept in late, grabbed a smoothie at a cool shop on her block, and explored districts of the Great City that she had never seen before.

When she got to work, everyone was very inviting and polite. They showed her the ropes – how to set up the camera, run the operating board, live stream the broadcast etc., but today, she was just in charge of operating one of the cameras. This wasn't a new or difficult task for her, since back in Orwell she was on the morning announcement broadcast team – the only difference being that the equipment here was much larger, more expensive, and *way* more up to date than what her small-town middle school could afford. She was excited to tell the boys about the experience – wondering how long their guard shift was going to last.

A couple of her fellow volunteers, Connor and Ashley, asked her to join them for dinner. They were a little bit older than her, maybe juniors or seniors in high school, but she didn't want to turn down a chance to make some new friends in the city, so she said yes. They went to a modern Asian restaurant with multi-colored mood lighting panels on the walls that would change color every minute or so. There weren't any buffets in the center of the dining area like she was used to. She also didn't see an option on the menu to order that sugar-coated donut that's always next to the jello at the buffet. She wasn't even sure what it was called, but she checked multiple times for it, only to come up disappointed.

"What brings you to Huxley?" Ashley asked. "Did your family move here?"

"No, me and my friends decided to come here." Ali replied.

"Oh, how come?" Ashley pursued.

Ali already felt a little out of place because of her age, and subsequently, her life experience gap. But on top of that, she didn't know how to even begin approaching the subject of a mythical creature sending her to the city to bring people back to West Virginia. "In this case," she thought, "it might be better just to lie."

"Well," she said to her dinner mates, "there's more to do here than in my hometown."

"Geez, tell me about it." Connor said. "I'm from Eschaton. Do you know where that is?"

"Yeah, kind of." Ali answered. "I know it's in West Virginia, but I've never been there. My friends are there right now."

"For real?" "He asked. "Man, tough luck for them."

Ali got a little worried. "How come?"

"Eh." Connor shrugged. "I don't know. Growing up there was just so boring. There were no events, shops, or anything like that. Everyone who lived there did their best to make me feel small even though they were small too. Now I just feel small because most of the people in Huxley don't know me. And in a way, I think that's better." He took a sip of his drink.

"Don't down on yourself." Ashley said in an attempt to comfort him. "You've made tons of friends and connections since you got here."

"Yeah, I guess." Connor replied. "Hey, your name is Ali, right?"

Ali nodded.

"Where are you from?" He asked.

"Um, Orwell..." She answered.

"Hot dog!" He said. "I've been to Orwell! Band competition junior year. Boy, you've got to know what I'm talking about with how there's nothing to do in West Virginia. I don't even think I saw a stoplight in your town!"

"Yeah, my friends and I mostly play video games and walk in the woods." She said, shyly.

"Well, that's about all you can do!" He replied.

"Are you from West Virginia, too?" Ali asked Ashley.

"Oh...no." She answered. "I'm from California. But I did live in good ole dub-vee for the first two years of high school before my family moved to Huxley."

"That's cool." Ali said. "I've never been to California."

"I wouldn't fantasize about it too much." Ashley warned. "It's okay. But remember that every place has its downsides. Sure, there's more to do out there, but anything you *could* do is just *so* expensive. Not to mention that there are so many people who will treat you like absolute garbage, *and* it's, like, also impossible to find some safe, drinkable water if the weather is bad. That's why I like Huxley. It's inexpensive, a beautiful city, and all the free and clean water anyone could ask for."

"That's great." Connor said to Ashley. "I didn't know you lived in West Virginia before you moved here, though."

"Yeah, but that's because you never ask me about myself...ever. All you care about is where we're going to eat and what movies are out this week."

"Hey, I ask about you sometimes!"

"Anyway..." Ashley said with a pause to let him know she was over their conversation, "Yeah, I lived in West Virginia for a bit. I'm glad I'm gone, though. It was kind of annoying for me to be there."

"Annoying how?" Connor asked, now trying to save face.

"It's just like..." She went on. "People literally *would not stop* asking me about California, like it was some golden land and that my entire value was wrapped up in my having lived there. But it's literally *just a place* – a place I couldn't wait to leave, either."

"That's how people in Orwell talk about our town." Ali added. "They can't stop talking about how much they hate it – about how they can't wait to win the lottery or have a genius kid that earns enough money to get them out of there. I think that's why they end up having so many kids...it increases their odds that one of 'em is gonna be a smart one."

Connor and Ashley chuckled at the judgment.

"That's a little sad, though." Ashley empathized. "Seems like both of us had crappy hometowns."

Connor put his chopsticks down, dramatically indicating that he had something to say.

"Ya know," he began, "I've thought about this quite a lot actually, and I think I've homed in on the secret." He looked up to make sure the girls were listening.

"Okay..." Ashley waited. "Out with it!"

"Everybody, everywhere, hates their hometown." He finally stated. "Maybe not completely, but it definitely seems like everyone has some kind of 'hometown syndrome' – where, at one time or another, they just can't wait to leave and go literally *anywhere* else. And I guess I get that. Like, if you grow up altogether in one town or state, that place is all you know. You've been grounded in one spot for so many years that all you can dream about is how far you can fly away. And you feel, although who knows how true that feeling may be, that the new place you'll go to *has* to be better than the place you're at now."

Connor quickly downed another bite of lo mein and continued.

"You know, I met some guy when I was on a study abroad trip to Greece." He continued. "The guy grew up in this one village and lived there his whole life, even raised a family there. And I mean this is in the middle of, like, picture-perfect Greece. Literally heaven on Earth. Mediterranean in front of you, mountains behind you, and enough rich history and culture to have a lifetime of fun. You know what he told me? Listen to this. He said it was his biggest wish to move to *Russia*. RUSSIA you guys...cold, desolate, gray Russia. I couldn't believe him when he said it. He said he was so used to living in paradise that it was boring to him. The vast nothingness of Russia was more appealing to him than a land most people DREAM of visiting even once before they die. Nothing against Russia, I suppose. It has its pros...probably...but I mean, come on...that's just crazy! Anyway, that's when I knew it was a universal experience for so many people. Whether it's West Virginia, Cali, or Greece, anyone who is born and raised in one place is bound to want to break out eventually - to mix things up. And good on them if they do. And good on them if they don't. Live your life the way you want to, I guess." He leaned back, stared at his noodles for a second, took a deep breath, then went back to eating.

Ali, somewhat stunned at the profundity coming from this man talking with a mouth full of food, wondered if his 'hometown syndrome' idea was actually true – if it was just so easy to get caught up in the negative aspects of the place you were raised in that it ends up sort of 'blinding' you to the negative aspects of other places, making them seem so much better than wherever you are from. Maybe focusing on all the bad that's around you also blinds you to all the good that's there, too. "Maybe that's why so many people leave West Virginia but end up coming back." She thought. "They leave, see that other places are riddled with just as many problems, then return home having more of an appreciation for where they grew up."

Everyone was taking in what Connor had just said. Ashley eventually let out a little chuckle, having humored herself in some way.

"What's up?" Connor asked.

"Well, you said that everyone dreams of going to the place opposite of where they're from." She noted.

"Yeah..." Connor awaited her explanation.

"Well, I just wondered…just where someone has to be from to dream of moving to West Virginia, other than the people who have actually lived or grown up there." She joked, clearly feeling a little sense of superiority.

"Maybe the Russians." Connor answered, playing along. "I'll ask em if I ever meet em. West Virginia really isn't that bad of a place, though." Connor took a break to inhale another portion of chicken. "It definitely blows in many ways, but there are far worse places to be."

As he said that, Ali felt a weird pull in her chest. Her stomach sank a little bit, and her eyes welled up. It was a weird feeling. All she could think about was her family. And Roxy. About how they must be worried sick. Then she thought of the boys, and whether or not they were okay. And while all of this was going on – while she was far away from everyone she loved – she was just sitting around, having dinner with people she didn't know in a strange city. She suddenly felt so alone, then anxious, and finally felt a quick urge to run away, although she wasn't sure where she would go.

"I have to go guys." Ali stated, hopping off the barstool and grabbing her things. "Thanks for inviting me. I'll see y'all tomorrow, okay?"

"Is everything okay?" Ashley asked, curious why their new friend was rushing off.

"Yeah, I'll be fine." Ali answered as she put some money on the table. "Tell the server to keep the change."

She forced a polite grin before hurrying out of the restaurant.

Ali stood outside and looked at the city. The whole thing was enclosed in concrete. She thought about how much she missed the sky. It was usually gray and cloudy where she was from, but it was still her sky. She felt a deep longing to go home, but she couldn't leave yet. What if the boys needed her help? What if they got in trouble? She knew she needed to stick around just in case. Then an idea dawned on her – a way she could see home, even if she couldn't go back just yet.

She took an elevator as high up as she could, then started looking for fire escape ladders, unmarked doors, or some way to get up to the roof of the dome. Eventually she opened a door to an emergency staircase that had a ladder leading up to a hatch in the roof. The hatch had a warning that said 'Only Open in Case of Emergency – Alarm Will Sound' but she figured the sign was bluffing, and she was right.

Ali swung the hatch open and pulled herself onto the roof. The concrete mass was lit up by the moonlight, just like the dense tree line below. As she looked down into the field next to the city, she could see little flying bugs that would glow on and off as they buzzed around. She remembered being a kid and trying to catch a bunch of them in a jar with her family at their house. Things were so much simpler back then. She wished she could go back to her house, but not the house she has now – the one she used to have – the house she knew before her parents got their promotions – before being inside watching TV was more appealing than sitting out in a field, catching lightning bugs.

From the roof, she could see faintly, in the distance, the bridge that she, Jake, and Noah rode over yesterday. So much had happened since then. She wished they were there with her, now. She thought about how much their group had changed in the time they had known each other.

Not even a couple years ago, she and her friends would find a way, consistently, to sneak out at night and do the stupidest activities just for fun. In just one night, they could come up with a dozen crazy ways to enjoy their time together – like going ghost hunting in the cemetery, buying a huge bag of those cheap freezer popsicles to see who could eat the most, or playing hide and seek in the neighborhood.

One time, the cops got called on them and they all tried to split to get away, but Noah got caught. She didn't see him for a while after that. She knew his dad was so mad at him, even though they were just trying to have fun.

But those nights just didn't happen anymore. They never went out at night like they used to. Now they just played video games in different houses, and she figured that wasn't so bad. In a way, they were still spending their time together, but it just wasn't the same as being together in person. She missed that so much. She missed them, her family, and how her life used to be.

She couldn't help but feel like she had lost so much joy in her life, like everything changed so slowly that she couldn't have even seen it coming. One less family outing here and there, a shop closing every few months, and before anyone could notice, life became still, even auto piloted in a way, like everybody was going through the motions waiting for life to happen to them sometime in the future, not realizing that it was happening to them right now. Everybody just did what they were supposed to do, passively, and never tried to make anything of it. She felt like so much of the life she loved had gone to waste, and it had never even occurred to her.

She began to cry, not just from the loss or the loneliness, but because her heart felt like it had been pulled out of her. She missed the home she knew was there but had been gone for years – the one that had a great community with fun activities and family days on the river and nighttime ice cream in the city. She wondered if everyone was to blame or just herself. Was her town and the people in it the reason life was so impersonal and meaningless or was it because she never ever made the effort to create her own meaning? Deep down she felt the latter was the truth, but maybe it was both.

Ali laid on the roof and continued crying for a while, until she eventually fell asleep under the stars.

· · · ● · ● · · · ·

"Child, are you okay?"

Ali jolted awake. It was like she heard that question in her dreams. There was an intense warmth coming from behind her, which didn't make any sense because it was still nighttime. There was a light hissing sound too. She turned around to see Nimkii, ablaze, floating a few yards behind her. Ali let out a quick, startled scream at the shock of seeing the cursed goddess.

"Oh my goodness, I'm so sorry. I'm so so sorry." Ali said, standing up quickly and adjusting herself, still waking up.

"It's okay. It's okay, dear." Nimkii reassured her. "What are you doing up here?"

"Oh...I just..." Ali looked around, feeling like she couldn't lie – like Nimkii could see right through her. She also realized that Nimkii had been speaking to her telepathically, just like the Mothman had. She wondered if the goddess had the ability to read her mind.

"I just needed some air." Ali explained. "I wanted a view. I've just been really homesick tonight."

"Oh." Nimkii comprehended. "Where are you from?"

"I'm from Orwell, West Virginia." Ali answered.

"Oh...well why on Earth are you missing it there?" Nimkii asked, surprised. "Is the city not making you happy? Tell me if there is a problem. I promise I will address it."

Ali felt very comfortable with Nimkii, despite how powerful and scary she was.

"No, no. The city is great." Ali reassured her.

"But surely something must not be right." Nimkii pushed. "I created the city. Please, tell me what needs to happen to make you happy and I will make it happen."

"It's just...I miss my family." Ali felt her eyes get heavy with sadness.

"Your family isn't here with you?"

"I was the only one who left. They still have to work back home."

"Well, what do they do for work?"

"They both work at the hospital. One is in surgery and the other is an administrator, so they're always really busy."

"Oh, honey." Nimkii said kindly. "Do you want them to live here with you? Is that what you want?"

"I just want us to be together again." Ali said, feeling the tears coming back to her eyes. "I don't know what happened."

"Say no more. We always need medical professionals in Huxley. I'll tell you what. I'll arrange for a train to take you back to Orwell in the morning. That way you can be together with them again. And, when you get there, tell your parents that if they are interested, I will pay for their tickets to move here, and jobs will be waiting for them when they arrive. If you love this town, the people you love should be here with you."

"Are you serious?" Ali asked in disbelief. "What if they don't want to move?"

"I'm very serious! And who wouldn't want to live here? Especially in comparison! But if that's the path they choose, you can always take the train back here free of charge, whenever you're ready. We'll make sure that, no matter what, you have a support system wherever you want to belong."

Ali was overwhelmed by Nimkii's generosity. "Thank you, Nimkii."

"When my people have joy, I have joy." The goddess explained. "Take as much time as you need. I'll fly down and alert the people at the station to prepare a train for you. It should be ready to go by morning."

Ali was overwhelmed by this act of kindness, and also incredibly happy to know that she would be able to see her family again very soon.

"Thank you so much, again." Ali repeated. "If I could give you a hug, I would."

"It's no problem at all." Nimkii responded kindly.

Ali turned to make her way down the hatch, but she paused for a moment and turned back toward Nimkii, who was flying toward the station.

"Hey, Nimkii!" Ali yelled.

The goddess stopped and turned to her.

"You really made an incredible city." Ali told her. "You've given everyone the chance to have an incredible life. You should be proud."

"Thank you, child." Her voice made it clear that Ali's words had impacted her. "You really don't know how much that means to me."

Ali gave Nimkii a smile and then made her way down the hatch and back toward the hotel – hoping to get some rest before the long trip home. Whenever the boys returned, she would ask them to take the train back with her. She honestly didn't care so much about the Mothman's quest any more. It was clear that Nimkii wasn't doing anything wrong – she was just trying to give everyone the life they deserve. That's why so many people were leaving the state – not because they didn't love it, but because other places existed that were more nurturing and kinder to them.

Ali wondered if Nimkii would let Noah and Jake's family move back for free, too, but realized that was probably asking too much. Jake loved living in Orwell, after all, and would probably never move. But still, Ali carried on dreaming that, one day, all of her people would be situated in one place, and that nobody would want to leave because they were all so happy being exactly where they were. She had never known a life like that, and she wasn't sure if she ever would.

Chapter Eight

THE THING THAT CALLS TO US

That night, Ali dreamt of a sunrise over the Appalachian hills. Beautiful swirls of gold and orange served as a backdrop to the deep, vivid tones of burgundy in the clouds. Above the tree line flew a little bird, heading straight for the horizon, silhouetted by the oncoming light.

The setting sun began to pulse arrhythmically, causing the sky to ripple with distortion.

Boom-Boom...Boom.

Boom-Boom...Boom.

The booms slowly transitioned into the sound of knocks as Ali woke up. The TV was still on in the hotel room. She leaned up and looked at it for a second, still coming-to. She figured she must have crashed on the couch after coming back from her late-night talk with Nimkii. She felt around the couch, then the floor, until she found the remote, and turned the TV off.

Knock-Knock...Knock.

A voice spoke from behind the door. "Ali, it's Noah. I lost my keycard."

Ali looked over at the door, realizing the knocks were not just from her dream, and sleepily hurried over to the door. She unbolted it, released the chain, and flung the door open to see her friend run in and give her a hug.

She was a little stunned by how quickly the whole sequence happened but was still relieved to see Noah safe and sound.

"Jesus H., dude." Ali said. "I was so worried about you all. Are y'all okay? Where's Jake?"

Noah released himself from the hug and took a deep breath, wiping his hand over his face as he turned to grab a glass of water from the kitchen area.

"He's outside, in the forest, with the horses. We figured it was too risky to take them inside."

Noah placed the glass under the faucet and tapped the touch-activated nozzle to begin pouring. He was dirty and had a blankness in his eyes.

"You look stressed. Did something go wrong?" Ali asked, just before her brain processed Noah's statement. "Wait, and you said you had horses?"

Noah leaned against the counter and took a long drink, wiping the excess water away from his mouth. Ali noticed the frail boyishness of her friend was no longer present. He was acting more mature, but also like he had just been through something deeply stressful.

He put the now-empty glass back on the table and looked at a 45-degree angle toward the ground, taking another long breath.

"Ali – I'm not gonna lie – it *freaking* sucked. But it was also, like, the coolest thing I've ever done. I don't know what to make of it. But yeah, we've got horses. And you'll never believe how we got 'em, either."

Ali was happy to see Noah have some emotion come back into his being, but her worry hadn't subsided.

"You didn't steal 'em, did ya?"

"No. But to be fair, I'm not exactly sure where they came from. I ain't ever seen horses like that before."

"Well, I wanna see em! And Jake. Is he okay?"

"Yeah, he's good too. I think we're both spazzing out though, thinking that the people from Eschaton or the guard will catch up to us. Cuz if they do, we're in big trouble."

"What the heck did you all do out there?"

"Ah, geez, Ali. It's too long to explain. And Jake's waitin' on us. We'll tell ya everything here in a bit. Are you doin' okay?"

"Yeah, I've just been hanging out. My shift at the media department was cool and pretty easy. Gah, I wish y'all had just stayed behind at this point."

"Yeah, that would've been nice, but we've got a good surprise waiting for you out there that we wouldn't have found unless we took the guard shift."

Ali grew curious and excited.

"Ooh, okay! I'm down for a surprise. Here, give me a quick sec to throw some new clothes on so we can go get Jake and catch up."

She shuffled over to the living area and began rummaging through what looked like shopping bags.

"Hey, do you mind if we stop for something to eat?" Noah asked. "I feel like Jake and I haven't had a real meal in days now. We've just been snacking on packaged crap."

Ali pulled a logoed Huxley hoodie over her head.

"Yeah, of course we can. I didn't eat much last night, anyway."

"Nice hoodie." Noah said. "Any new discoveries yesterday?"

Ali was putting on her socks and shoes.

"Oh, yeah. Tons of stuff. I actually have a surprise for you all, too. We'll have to see which one is more shocking."

Noah let out a a playfully pompous laugh. "Alright...but don't be mad when Jake and I win!"

Ali looked up at him with a jestful glare before returning to tying her shoes.

"Well, I guess we'll just have to see when we cross that bridge, won't we?"

"Heh. Guess so."

Ali took all of her possessions with her, not sure if housekeeping was going to clean out the room before they got back. She and Noah then made their way to an elevator and asked Penny to take them to the train station.

· · · · ● · ● · · ·

As they walked onto the platform, Ali noticed one lonely train sitting at the station, swallowed up by a dense fog. She wondered if that was her train or someone else's. She hoped it was hers.

Visibility was low. The tops of the trees poked through the surrounding fog. Other than that, the only thing the kids could see were a couple of guards stationed along the city's walls.

"Which direction Jake?" She asked.

Noah pointed to the left of the train. "He's out there. A bit deeper into the forest."

"Okay." She replied.

They walked off the station's platform and began venturing into the misty woods. After a couple minutes of walking, Ali saw the outline of a short-statured kid with curly hair, flanked by two horses.

"Noah, there he is!" She said, as she took off in a run to see her friend.

"I see you, girl!" Jake shouted. "I better be gettin' a hug!"

Ali slowed her jog as she neared her friend and gave him a big hug, picking him up and swinging him around.

"Geez, you tree, put me down! I ain't a baby!"

Ali laughed as she continued to swing him around.

"Look, Noah! I caught me a baby!"

Jake tried to wriggle himself free, to no avail.

Noah laughed as he continued walking closer to his friends.

Ali, with Jake in her arms, had a big smile on her face. She looked over at the ground next to them, making sure she didn't run into anything while she was rotating. That is when she saw an open bag carrying a severed head.

"What the heck!" Ali yelled as she stepped backwards, lost her balance, and slipped on the leaves, falling flat on her back with Jake crashing on top of her.

"Oh snap!" Noah said to himself as he rushed over to help them out.

Ali threw Jake off of her and squirmed away from the bag.

"What is that?!"

Noah walked over and tried to calm her.

"Ali."

"Noah, what is that?!" She was staring at the bag as if the head was going to crawl out and chase her at any second.

"Remember how we were debating who had the bigger surprise?"

Ali looked up at Noah quickly, then back at the bag. "What? Um, yeah..."

"I think I win." Noah stated with pride.

"That's not a good surprise, though! Why do you have a human head in a bag?!"

Jake walked over and helped Ali up.

"It *is* a good surprise, Ali. And it's not human." Jake pointed toward the bag. "*That's* Kanati."

Ali looked over at Jake, then at Noah, who gave a confirming nod.

"But...what...how do you guys know that? He's dead."

"I'm not dead." Kanati spoke from the bag.

"Jesus Christ!" Ali yelled as she felt her heart skip a beat. "H...*oh* my god." She grabbed onto her chest, leaned forward, and began breathing heavily – having been sufficiently spooked.

"It's okay, it's okay." Jake tried to calm her. "We found him in Eschaton and rescued him."

"Hold on." Ali requested, lowering her head, and giving a 'please wait' index finger.

Jake gave her a couple pats on the back. "Been there, buddy. Been there."

She stood straight again and took a deep breath.

"Okay, so you all stole the head of a god that we *thought* was dead from the town, and now you're worried they're looking for you?"

"Oh, they're definitely looking for us. But yeah, that's the gist."

"But...I thought you all were just like...watching over an event or something easy like that."

"Yeah, *big* misunderstanding on our part." Noah admitted. "But look at the bright side, now we have something to bring back to Ani. Imagine how excited he'll be to have his dad back. And how much that will help his cause!"

"I mean," Ali started, "you definitely have to fill me in on how this whole thing went down, but I'm starting to think that this might work out *very* conveniently for us."

"How do you mean?" Jake wondered.

"Well, last night, I kind of had an unexpected encounter with Nimkii. Talked to her and everything."

"What?!" Jake exclaimed. "For real?"

"For real for real."

"Holy frick. That's terrifying."

"Actually not really."

"No?"

"I mean...at first, yeah. But you'd be surprised. She's, like, *extremely* thoughtful and down-to-earth. When she found out I was feeling home-sick, she prepared a train for me to come home. Noah, you know the train that was at the station? I think that was mine."

"No way." Noah reacted. "Can all three of us take it?"

"I have to imagine so. But we can check."

"Wait wait wait." Jake interjected. "We have a free-and-clear train to go home, with no other passengers on board?"

"Um...yeah." Ali was curious. "Why?"

"Ohh that's actually *perfect*. The Gods of Old have looked kindly upon us today!"

Ali giggled at her silly friend. "How so?"

"Okay, okay." He started. "Just think about this. If we stick around here much longer, they're going to catch us with Kanati, right? Which means we gotta get outta dodge, like, *today*."

"Right..." Noah prodded.

"Well, that's not all. Let's not forget why we're here – to bring Huxleyans back to West Virginia. And quite honestly...I can't help but see a golden opportunity sitting right in front of us with this train."

"Ah, geez, man." Ali moaned. "I'm sorry, but I don't know about that...the people here look pretty happy. They're just living their lives and doing their thing. I love Ani and everything...but I just don't see why we need to be causing any kind of commotion about this. Can't we just leave them alone?"

"I'm with Ali, here." Noah seconded.

"But..." Jake thought. "But we promised Ani we would help him."

Noah sighed, knowing Jake had a good point. He looked over at Ali.

"I don't know. What do you think?" He asked her.

Ali let out an annoyed grunt. "Give me a sec." She stood there in contemplation. "You wanna walk into the city with your friend over there?" She asked, gesturing toward Kanati.

"Ah, crap." Noah got her point. "You're right." He thought for a moment. "Do you think we can drop him off on the train? Nobody would think to look there."

Jake looked over toward the bag.

"Kanati, would that be okay?"

"As long as I am sufficiently hidden, that will be fine." Kanati answered. "I don't want a chance of them finding me."

"Don't worry, we'll try to be quick too." Jake added.

"In that case…" Ali let out a sigh. "Fine. Let's get in there, get you all some food, and come up with a game plan. But only on one condition."

"Hit me." Jake requested.

"We have to leave by the afternoon *at the latest*. Deal?"

"You had me at food." Noah answered.

"Good." Ali said. "Now, let's go drop Kanati off and see how long we have the train for. What's the plan with the horses?"

"We'll, I guess we're gonna have to send them back to wherever they came from." Noah said. "Kanati?"

"I can help with that." The godhead spoke.

"But…wait." Jake said with a whine. "Are you sure? I really like mine."

"Awh, buddy, it'll be okay." Noah comforted his friend. "They've finished their job with us. We have to let them be free."

"Yeah…you're right." Jake understood. "I'm just sad that they're going…"

Noah walked over to the satchel.

"Kanati, we're ready when you are."

A deep hum began resonating from the bag, once again vibrating the air around them. The horses immediately turned and began to gallop back toward their land.

"Okay, so that's freaking cool." Ali said.

"Yeah, no way that's gonna get old." Noah replied.

There was a pause as the friends stared off at the horses, watching them fade into the dense forest fog. Once they were a good ways off, Ali broke her gaze.

"Alright y'all, food time?" Ali asked. "Well, with a pit stop at the train station first?"

"Absolutely." Noah confirmed. "I'm starving."

The three friends gathered their things and made their way back to Huxley's train depot, where Ali confirmed that the train was, in fact, theirs, and that they would be leaving before the end of the day.

From there, they headed toward a burger joint Jake had eyed on their first day in the city. Once there, they ordered smorgasbord of sliders and sides and began catching each other up on all that had happened while they were away from each other. It was the first time since their journey began that they felt like they had a moment to just be themselves.

When the burgers were gone, they doubled back for ice cream. Jake got Rocky Road, his favorite, Ali a graham cracker s'mores cone, and Noah a fudge sundae. At that point, the group knew it was time to come up with a plan for what they were doing next.

"So how in the world are we gonna recruit people to go back to West Virginia?" Noah asked his friends. "This place is *actually* massive, and we don't have a lot of time."

"I'm not exactly sure." Ali said as she was trying to deal with the bottom of the cone dripping melted ice cream on her hand. "I have kind of a wild idea, but I think there's a chance that we're early enough to where it just might work."

"Wild idea? You already know I'm in." Jake affirmed.

"Okay," Ali looked up at her friends, "so...I have keycard access to the media department where they broadcast stuff to the city's televisions."

Jake's eyes lit up in realization of what she was saying. "You're a genius." He said.

"What if," Ali laughed as she went on, "we snuck in there this morning and put out some sort of video to everyone's TVs? They showed me how to do it yesterday. I'm just not sure how many people will be watching right now. I know it's early in the day for a TV broadcast, but I think it's *way* better than walking around and asking people individually."

"I actually think that idea is brilliant." Noah said. "But like, are you allowed to do that?"

Ali snorted a little bit in laughter. "Oh, there's *no chance* that I'm allowed to do that. But, like, I don't see a better option."

"What if we get caught, though?" Noah worried. "You might not be able to come back here with your family if you get in trouble."

"Shoot, that's true." Ali realized. "I don't know, it's not *that* bad of a thing to do, right? And Nimkii's really cool. I'm sure she would completely understand."

"Here's what I'm worried she *won't* understand." Noah began to inquire. "How do you expect her to react when she finds out we are working with her estranged brother, trying to steal people away from *her city*? I don't know about you two, but to me, I ain't messin' around with a fire monster that can shoot lightning out of her hands."

"Ah, crap." Jake said, removing the ice cream away from his face for a moment. "I hadn't even thought about that. She's gonna zap us."

"She ain't gonna zap us..." Ali defended. "She's got a good heart – trust me. However, I *am* worried about her brother showing up here unannounced. Do you know for sure that he's coming?"

"Honestly, I have no clue." Jake answered. "We don't know if my messenger bird ever even found him. I guess the only way we'll know is if Ani shows up out of the blue. And if we're lucky, Nimkii won't mind him being here."

"Or, if we're *really* lucky," Noah added, "she won't find out in the first place."

"Yeah, that would be nice." Jake agreed. "They've definitely got some unresolved stuff going on."

After finishing their cones, they took turns going to the restroom to wash the sugar off their hands and faces. When they were all back together, Ali asked, "okay, are y'all ready to try this media department stunt?"

"I don't know if I'm ready for fame..." Jake started. "But I think it's ready for me."

Ali laughed. "Come on boys. Let me show you the studio."

They stood up, left burger place, and walked over to the nearest elevator, which led them up to the broadcasting station's level. From there, they walked down one of the elevated streets until Ali stopped at a glass entrance door that had the media department's logo decaled on it. Behind the glass panes were some aluminum blinds, but it was clear that no lights were on inside.

"It's still pretty early in the morning." Ali told the boys, "so nobody should be stopping by until later today. But try to keep an eye out anyway in case someone walks by."

She scanned her keycard and the door unlocked. They snuck inside and the boys sat around while Ali slowly guessed how to turn on all the equipment. After a stint of messing around with the buttons on the board, she finally got the live feed set up and turned on the TV monitors. After that, she went over to a video camera that was secured to a tripod and set it up so they could stand in front of it to broadcast their message.

"Do we need to rehearse or something?" Noah asked nervously, worried about sounding stupid in front of the entire city.

"I don't know." Ali kept working, still worried someone might stop by at any moment and catch them. "Just talk about what happened. Tell the truth. You'll be fine. Y'all go ahead and stand in front of the camera. I want to make sure the shot's good."

The boys stood in front of the camera awkwardly, not sure where to look.

"Okay, when I hit this big red button, we're going live to every TV that's turned on in the city." Ali informed them. Do you all need anything before I hit this button?"

"I just wanna say that if we get caught – I love you guys." Jake told them.

Ali and Noah gave closed, fond smiles toward him. "We'll be okay." Ali reassured him. "You ready?"

"I can't be less ready...but screw it. Let's go." Jake said.

"Okay." Ali prepped them. "Three. Two. One."

She hit the 'LIVE' button, which played a short intro graphic of 'Huxley TV' choreographed with a news-like tune. This bought her enough time to hustle over to where the boys were standing. When the graphic whipped off the screen, it revealed the three middle schoolers, standing awkwardly but bravely in front of the camera.

"Jake, you go first." Ali whispered, tapping her friend with her hand.

"I don't know what to say." Jake whispered back aggressively.

The red 'Live' light was staring at all three of them, adding more and more pressure to say something.

Everyone was panicking internally, but Noah realized that if someone didn't say something soon, any potential viewer they had would lose interest. So, with a gulp of bravery, he forced out the words, "Um, hi, everyone. Our names are Noah, Ali, and Jake. We're from Orwell, West Virginia. And, um, we're here because the Mothman asked us to be here. He, um, wants us to ask you all for something. He wants us to see if any of you want to come back, with us, to revitalize West Virginia."

Noah looked at his friends, begging them with his strained stare to say something.

"You see," Jake started, "the three of us love where we're from. It ain't as nice as what you all have here, but there are some beautiful things in our state that you just can't find in a place like this."

"Yeah." Noah stepped in. "Things like bonfires, small little mom-and-pop-type stores, late night drives through the woods, and just those simple kinda things that life is all about."

Ali, in her heart, knew that Nimkii and Huxley had been nothing but kind to them, and that speaking now would be spitting in their faces, but something deeper within her felt like she was called to speak at this moment – to help the town and the people that had spent their time raising her and supporting her.

"Exactly." Ali braved. "Here in Huxley, you have every luxury imaginable. There's no denying the prosperity and good fortune being in a city like this could afford you, but for anyone listening to this who is from West Virginia, don't you just feel that tear in your heart every time you think of home? I crossed that border not two days ago, and my heart feels like it's been ripped out of my chest ever since. Gosh, I don't know what that feeling is...it's like something I yearn for even though I can't quite describe it. It's something that keeps calling to me, begging me to come home."

"To me," Jake took the baton, "the thing that calls me home is our home-town biscuit restaurant. And getting to see my grandma every Sunday, seeing how happy it makes her to be with her family. Actually, it's just my entire family that calls to me. It's only been two days, and I already miss being around them so much."

"For me," Noah joined Jake's line of thought, "that thing is my friends, and how, despite some of the terribleness I have to deal with back there, they are always there for me. They have my back, and I try to have theirs."

Jake looked over at his friend with gratitude and hugged him. "So you're sayin' I don't annoy you too bad?"

"Not enough." Noah joked.

Jake and Noah looked over at Ali, waiting for her to say the thing that calls her back home.

"For me," Ali looked up, thinking for a moment, "it's...my comfort." She let out a little laugh of realization. "From what I've heard and seen during my two days here, Huxley has every sort of comfort imaginable. But...I guess that's not the kind of comfort I'm talking about. This comfort is one that comes from...inside. It's not about having nice technology or cool buildings or anything like that; it's about having a home, no matter how big or small, and knowing that you belong there. And it's not a house, either. My home exists where the people I love are, and that's why it's honestly so dang hard to go anywhere else."

"Ain't that the truth." Jake followed up. "I can handle short blips away from West Virginia, but honestly, I can't imagine leaving long-term. But tons of people do anyway...so what does that mean? I've wondered a lot if I've been wrong all this time. After all, I'm definitely in the minority way of thinking here that it's not only plausible but *totally possible* to live and be happy in your hometown. And I get that some people have bad blood with where they're from, but at the end of the day, I think for most people it's a matter of perspective."

"What do you mean?" Ali asked, unsure of where her friend was trying to take this line of thought.

"I mean...that people feel the need to live complex lives..." He paused. "Yeah! That's it. There's this sort-of existential push that makes *so* many people feel like if they don't lead enough of a complex, busy, and dynamic life – that if their lives are just filled with the same people and the same places and the same restaurants – that they have somehow 'failed' at life. I don't know where that comes from...but whatever it is...I don't have it. And it's really funny to me because most people know that life is made up of the simple things – like watching a sunset, getting ice cream with your dad, or driving around doing stupid stuff with your friends. So...why do we feel the need to keep abandoning the things we know we like, or the things we find comfortable and familiar, just to feel like our lives weren't wasted? Would you say that a person who spent their life being with the people they loved and loving others was a wasted one? All because they never lived in New York or traveled to Machu Picchu? Imagine the kind of life you could have if, instead of thinking that this time we have on Earth is a game of 'who can collect the most passport stamps and pay the highest rent', you played the game of 'finding *total* joy and meaning by taking your grandma to the farmer's market'. Do you see what I mean? Imagine having that level of comfort within yourself and your own life that you can go support a local musician who has a $5 cover charge and *completely* enjoy your evening, all while making that artist's night, without *once* thinking about how that musician is nowhere close to being as talented or as popular as whatever megastar is rolling through town next week."

He turned to his friends. "Are you all seeing what I'm saying?"

As Jake looked deeper into his friends' eyes, he saw a sense of shattering in them. He panicked a bit, realizing that nobody was talking.

"Guys?"

Noah, still in a trance from Jake's words, looked over at his friend as a tear plummeted from his eye.

"Um, Jake." Noah wiped his cheek. "You have a gift; do you know that?"

Jake grew bashful. "I don't know what you mean."

"I mean…that if I had even *half* the amount of security that you feel in your life, I would consider myself extremely lucky."

"Really?"

"Yeah, man. Really. I go through, every day, wishing I was somewhere else or doing something completely different. I wish I wasn't in school, eating cheap food, or stuck in a town with nothing to do. But, man, you have so much peace in your heart that you don't mind all of that…"

"Well, if I may…" Jake interrupted. "It's not that I don't notice the food is crappy or that our town is boring – it's that I don't *care* about any of that, as long as I'm with the people I love. And I love the heck outta you guys. We could eat rocks for all I care, and I'd still be happy. Toothless, but happy."

"Awh, buddy." Noah said as he walked over and gave Jake a hug. Ali smiled at her friends being cute just before snapping back to the reality that they were on camera.

"Sorry, everyone." She said. "We got sidetracked. But I think this is the exact point we are trying to make. If you want to live in a place where the people around you prioritize the little things, please, come back with us to West Virginia – a place where you won't be judged by what car you drive or the fact that you wore your pajamas to the grocery store today."

"Yeah, if anything, you would be overdressed." Noah joked.

Ali smacked him on the chest.

"What?" Noah lightheartedly defended with a laugh. "You've been to the grocery stores."

"Okay, good point." Ali said with a smile. "Anyway, we know that we're just middle schoolers, and that you all probably have jobs and families and lives that you've built here. So we're not gonna stand here and act like you all will just up and leave something that you've established. I guess that we're just asking you to think about it. And, in time, if you want to join us, we'll be happy to have you."

"Or," Jake jumped in, "if you're feeling really ambitious, you can join us today."

"Yeah, that's right!" Ali said. "We..." She noticed a person's silhouette passing by the aluminum blinds. She stopped talking to watch the shadow as it approached the station's doorway. Noah and Jake looked over at her, saw the worry on her face, and also looked toward the door.

"Crap." She said. "Guys, we gotta go."

"Um, um...wait...you gotta finish what you were saying." Jake hurried. "About the train."

"Uhhhhh...right!" Ali realized, still in a panic as two more silhouettes passed by the window. "We have a train leaving for Orwell today. You all can totally join. Anyway, we gotta skedaddle, but let's meet there at...um..." She looked up at the station's clock. It read 11:36. "Four o'clock. The train will leave at four o'clock. Okay, bye everyone!"

She ran out of frame and over to the control panel, shutting off the live feed just as the door swung open and the media department manager walked in with two police officers.

"Split up!" Jake commanded to his friends, who immediately began ducking under furniture and running to opposite sides of the room in order to confuse the cops.

"Hey!" The manager yelled. "Stop!"

Jake and Noah were trying to juke the officers. Ali crouched behind the operating board, looking for a chance to break out, but the manager was blocking the doorway.

"Kids, stop! Now!" The manager commanded. His voice stilled the energy in the chaotic room. Everyone, including the police officers, stood in place, and looked back at him. The manager let out a stressful sigh.

"Listen, guys. You can't be in here." The man said calmly. "Leave peacefully, and we won't have any problems. I don't want trouble. I just want you guys to get out."

Ali, Noah, and Jake were happy to hear such a reasonable solution. Ali, whose heart was about to collapse from worry that she was finally going to get in trouble, stood up from her hiding spot. "Really?" She asked, still a little guarded.

"Yes, really." The manager had his hands on his waists, clearly stressed, but not necessarily angry. "You're the new volunteer, right?"

"Yeah...." Ali said to him with regret. "I'm sorry, I was the one who snuck us in..." She held out the keycard and walked over to hand it to him.

"Thank you for giving me that." He looked down at her. "Listen, I was young once and did stupid stuff, too. But there's no reason to ruin anyone's lives over it. Does everyone feel like they learned a lesson, here?"

"Oh, yessir." Jake stated.

"Definitely." Noah agreed.

"We had good intentions." Ali told the man. "I really don't feel good about it, but you won't have to worry about us anymore." She looked over at the officers. "You two won't, either. I promise."

"Okay, if you promise," the manager said, feeling like his lesson had been sufficiently dealt, "then have a good day." He stepped out of the doorway.

Ali looked at her friends. "Come on, boys." She said to them. They hustled over to her. As the trio walked out of the studio, each of them thanked the manager and the guards for their mercy. The officers exited with the kids and followed them for a while, making sure there wouldn't be any more issues. After a few minutes, the officers broke off and walked in a different direction. The manager stayed behind and began setting everything up for the afternoon broadcast.

Ali, Noah, and Jake got into an elevator and asked Penny to close the doors.

Once the doors were closed and the kids knew they were in the clear, they all let out a huge sigh of relief. Noah put his head against the elevator's glass and closed his eyes. Ali and Jake plopped to the floor.

"Oh my *god*." Jake put his hands on his face. "I thought we were *screwed*."

"Yeah, me too." Ali said. "I don't think you guys could have gotten around the guards."

"Maybe one of us...not all of us." Noah figured. His eyes were still closed.

"Well, it worked out regardless." Ali noted. "I hope at least a few people saw our speech..."

"Heck, if the media guy saw it...I figure other people did, too." Noah opened his eyes and realized the elevator wasn't moving. "Guys, are we gonna take this elevator anywhere?"

"Probably." Ali said. "I panicked and said they should meet us at four. I was so worried we were gonna be detained or something like that. But that means we gotta kill some time now."

"Jake, any suggestions?" Noah asked his friend, who was still facepalming, coming down from the excitement.

"Penny." Jake's voice was muffled from his hands. "Take us to the movie theater."

The elevator played a confirming sound and began moving.

"I need a place to relax, get some food, and forget about things for a bit." Jake told his friends.

"I feel that." Ali agreed. "Noah, how about you pick the movie."

"Well, I'm sure I could find something interesting that's out." Noah reckoned. "But y'all gotta want to see it, too."

"Sounds good." Jake lifted his face out of his hands. "I'm not picky."

"I really do wonder if our speech worked, though." Ali questioned.

"We did well." Noah said. "And we did all we could. Now we just have to wait and see if it pays off."

CHAPTER NINE

THE GREAT APPALACHIAN REDEMPTION

"What did y'all think?" Noah asked as they were leaving the movie theater.

"Eh, it was alright." Ali said. "I'm kind of getting tired of superheroes, or at least *those* superheroes..."

"Same." Jake seconded, taking a deep sigh. "I don't know..." He looked off, lost in thought for a moment. "I just feel like I always know what's going to happen...and somehow that kills it for me. Even if the story is exciting, I'm never that worried about the heroes."

"Why not?" Ali asked him.

"I mean...isn't it just obvious that the bad guy will *never* win, and that the hero will *always* make it out okay, no matter what?" Jake answered. "It's apparent to me the whole time I'm watching because, in the end, I know the studios want to milk as much money out of these superheroes as they can. So even if those heroes *are* threatened with some kind of dire consequences, they'll *always* find a way to win – either by some deux ex machina scenario or time travel or some other nonsense. I don't know –

it just makes it hard for me to buy into the plot when I already know the stakes are just an illusion..."

"Yeah, I'm actually 100% with you there." Ali agreed. "I'm not saying that I really *want* to see tragedy in a fun action film, but yeah, at least sell me on the consequences – wrap me into the story. But even more than that, what really takes me out of it is actually the special effects."

"Like, too many special effects?" Noah asked.

"Yeah..." Ali clarified. "I mean, it's a superhero movie – I get that – so it's going to have crazy-looking characters who need to shoot lightning out of their hands or something, but like, do we really need all of these worlds and universes and stuff? I think I would prefer more human-focused stories that *involve* superheroes – not these big 'gods versus titans' kind of overproduced flicks, if that makes sense."

"No, you're right. That makes sense." Noah confirmed, taking a pause to think. "Well, I guess the idea is that if the movie isn't going to be good, at least it'll be pretty."

Ali laughed a bit. "That checks out." She leaned over a railing and looked down at the Great City below, getting lost in a gaze, thinking about something else.

"Somethin' on your mind, Ali?" Noah looked over the railing to see if she was looking at something specific, but he didn't see anything. Her eyes were caught in the lights, lost in a daydream.

"Yeah." She answered. "I just think it's crazy."

"What's crazy?" He pursued.

"That we're here." Ali answered. "That we have this fun and exciting life standing right in front of us. It's something we've always dreamt of, and now we're about to walk away from all of it." She paused. "I don't know, maybe we're going to walk away because there's something deeper than just having an exciting life."

"Or maybe we're just a bunch of suckers." Noah half-joked, looking at Ali.

Ali chuckled. "Yeah, that could be it, too."

"We haven't done too bad for ourselves in the adventure department this week, despite being a bunch of rubes." Jake joked. "But I don't think leaving this city is something for us to mourn. There might be some wisdom in not hanging on to the thrill of it all too tightly – ya know? Maybe there's wisdom in letting things go when it is their time to go – knowing that something else will pop up later."

"Dang." Ali reacted, lifting her head up a bit, feeling better. "Yeah, I think that might be it. I think it's time for me to let this city go, at least for now, and head home to my family."

Noah smiled and gave Ali a side hug. Jake joined in. Together they took one last look at the Great City of Huxley, with all of its innovations and dancing lights, and said their own goodbyes to it, not knowing if they would see it again.

"Come on." Noah told his friends. "It's time to see if anyone heard our message."

They took the elevator over to the train station. As they walked outside of the city's walls, they noticed the fog had cleared and that it was a beautiful day. They looked around the platform, trying to see if anyone was awaiting their arrival. Some people were scattered around, but there definitely wasn't a crowd. Inside themselves, the trio felt a little let down, hoping their words had caused some sort of mass movement, which they clearly hadn't.

"Kid's, look!" They heard a man call out in their direction as he tapped the shoulders of his children to catch their attention. "These people are the ones from the TV this mornin'!"

"Woah!" The man's daughter exclaimed, staring in amazement at the friend group. She looked back at her dad. "Can I go say hi?"

"Well, of course you can!" The dad told her. The little girl took off running toward Ali, Noah, and Jake, who were a little surprised that they were recognized.

"Hi, I'm Daphne." The little girl said, very properly. "Did you like being on the TV?"

Ali smiled at the little girl's cuteness and bent down to talk to her. "Yeah, we did!" She answered. "It was really scary at first, but it got easier once we started talking."

"That's awesome." Daphne said. "You're really pretty."

Ali's heart melted. "Awh, thank you, Daphne. You're really pretty too. I love your boots."

Daphne looked down and gave a proud smile. "Thank you!" She said.

"We really liked what y'all had to say this mornin'." The father told the group as he was walking up with his wife and son to greet the kids. He reached out for a handshake. "Dan Neubraman." He turned to his family. "This is my wife, Jordan, our son, Brendan, and of course you've met Daphne." He pointed at the train. "Is this the train to go back?"

"Um, yeah." Ali answered, still a little stunned by the reality that someone was there to join them. "You all want to come back to Orwell with us?"

"Well, yeah!" Jordan confirmed. "We're actually from there, and my mom still lives there. We've been thinkin' about goin' back for some time now. I guess your little speech was just the exact push we needed."

"Exactly." Dan agreed, leaning in for a whisper. "And these train ticket prices are *excessive*, especially with four people, so it would've been stupid to pass up on the opportunity for a free ride. We packed as fast as we could."

"Well, I'm glad you all are here." Ali led, though her suspicion had not subsided yet. "I am curious, though." She continued, gesturing toward Daphne and her brother. "Aren't they in school right now? I don't mean to butt in to y'all's personal lives, but I guess I just didn't expect to see a family up and move like this."

"Ah, don't worry about that, honey." Jordan returned. "Moving schools is tough, but the kids have plenty of friends at home they can play with, so the transition won't be so bad."

"Oh, that's nice."

"Yeah! Truth is that we have no shortage of reasons to take everyone back home. We have an absolutely *huge* support system there that we are desperately lacking in the city. I mean, do you know how much childcare costs *each day*, for *two kids* in Huxley? More than most people can afford...I can tell you that...at least if they want to eat once a day."

"Dang."

"Dang indeed." Dan added. "We've got tons of family and friends in Orwell who want to help look after Daphne and Brendan, so it's not a big problem.

Plus, we're feeling just a *little* cramped fitting our four-piece family in a tiny little city apartment."

"Gosh, ain't that the truth." Jordan agreed. "I could use a room to myself, no offense baby."

"No, I get it." Dan understood. "Me too, me too."

"The land is just so dang cheap back home" Jordan continued. "So we're lookin' to get a nice little house with some land, maybe even fence in a little section of it so we can finally get the kids a "d.o.g.".

Daphne closed her eyes really tight, trying to decipher her mom's message. A couple seconds later, she opened her eyes, having figured out the word.

"Mom! Mom!" She yelled, tugging at Jordan's pantleg. "We're getting a dog?"

Jordan laughed and bent down to talk to her. "Maybe! If we can find a nice house with a yard!"

"Can we get a bulldog?" Daphne wondered. "I like their squishy faces."

Jordan laughed. "I'll talk to your dad about it and we'll let you know."

"Are y'all the Mothman people?" A gravelly voice shouted from behind the family. The whole group turned to see a middle-aged man, who was wearing a rain jacket and a ball cap, walking toward them.

"Yessir, we are!" Jake yelled back.

"Good!" The man replied. He walked closer to the group but still kept a bit of distance, looking off toward the train. "I'm Mark Horn. I'm thinkin' about joinin' ya." His voice was very loud and firm.

"Oh, good!" Ali remarked. "These are the Neubramans. They'll be joining us."

"Howdy folks." Mark raised his ball cap in respect before securing it back on his noggin. "Now, before I get on this here train, how do I know you kids ain't crazy?"

"What do you mean, sir?" Noah inquired.

"I mean, I was impressed by your bravery to ask people to come back to West Virginia with ya, but I don't buy that Mothman bit." Mark explained. "I'm a believer myself, but I guess I just don't see why he would, for one, want to *help* the state he terrorizes, and two, would enlist a bunch of kids to do his bidding! Seems a little farfetched to me – maybe even cult-like. I just can't help but suspect that you kids are tryin' to trick us or somethin'."

"We're telling the truth, sir. I promise." Jake defended. "We actually met the Mothman. He's not that scary once you know him. I know it sounds a little crazy to say out loud, but I have some proof that he sent us, if you want it."

"You do?" Mark wondered. "Alright, let's see it, then." This man was definitely one of the conspiratorial types, always suspecting collusion and bad intentions before anything else. "But," he went on, "you better not tell me you have a picture of the Mothman or nothin' like that. I've seen way too many 'photos of proof' in my lifetime...and they're all a bunch of fakes, I can tell you that right now."

"It's not a picture." Jake clarified. "But if you want proof, you can come with me on the train, and I'll show ya."

"Yeah, I suspect that'll do." Mark agreed, walking over to join Jake, who turned to his friends.

"Okay, guys, I'll be right back." He said as he led Mark onto the train to show him Kanati.

They were just about to step onto the train when a female voice called toward them from a distance.

"Are we too late, Mark?!" The woman said, hurriedly walking with her friend onto the platform."

"All good, Abigail!" Mark yelled back, turning away from the train, and his evidence hunt, so he could go greet them. "One of these kids was just about to show me some proof that the Mothman sent them."

"Oh, honey, you don't need that stuff." The woman said, waving her hand as if to dismiss his notion. She held out her arms and wrapped him in a hug. "That's not the real reason we're going back anyway, now, is it?"

"Well, I reckon not." Mark realized. "But you can't be too careful."

"You're *all* coming?" Ali asked, surprised to see more people show up.

"Well heck yeah, girl!" Abigail yelled. "We seen what you was doin' on the TV this mornin' and I said to my friend, 'girl, it is time for us to get outta here and settle down.' Besides, I think we're a little too *country* for this place anyhow, but we didn't have much of a choice in movin' here originally becuz this is where the work was."

"Oh." Ali processed. "Well, what are you gonna do for work back home, then?"

"Ah shoot, I don't know." She replied. "We'll figure it out. I've got connections for days down there. It might not be the same money, but I'll learn to make do."

As she said that, there was a rumble in the sky.

"What the heck is thunder doin' out on a day like this?" Abigail asked, looking up. "There ain't hardly a cloud in the sky."

Ali, Noah, and Jake's eyes opened wide. They ran to the edge of the platform to get a better view above them. The other passengers looked at them in confusion.

"What do y'all suspect?" Mark asked, peering up with the others.

With the group's eyes fixed on the sky, looking away from the city, a loud rush of air came from behind them as the Mothman passed over the dome and into their vision.

"Woah, Jesus..." Mark reacted as the wind blew the cap off his head.

Daphne screamed at the sight and ran behind her mom's legs, looking between them to see what was going on from a place of protection.

Jake's eyes lit up with joy at the sight of his friend. He gave a couple celebratory jumps, swinging his arms in the air. "The cardinal found him!" He looked back with a smile. "Guys, my idea worked!"

The future passengers watched as Ani flew in circles above them. It was amazing how fast he could fly.

"Ani! Ani!" Jake yelled as he waved one of his arms back and forth, then looked back at his friends. "Guys, I'll be back in a second." He darted over to the old train and climbed up its ladder.

"Well call me a fool..." Mark uttered in disbelief. "I do believe that's him..." He gave a slight smile at the sight.

"Ani! Down here!" Jake yelled, waving his arms from the top of the train.

The Mothman, seeing the signal below, closed his wings and performed another dive-bomb-like drop in the sky. Just before he reached the station, the monster opened his wings and broke his momentum – which sent a crack of air rippling across the region – as his talons landed with a big thud on top of the train. The force of air from his landing was so strong that it rocked the vehicle and sent the Neubraman family's luggage flying backwards. Everyone close by had to take a couple steps back to brace themselves against the strong gust of wind.

Nearby, the Huxleyan guards were watching the beast in horror, unsure of what to do.

Jake ran across the grated train top and gave Ani a quick hug before backing away. The onlookers were shocked that he approached the large, hideous creature so haphazardly. "I didn't think you'd show!" Jake said to his friend.

"How did you get that message to me?" The Mothman's voice spoke only to Jake.

"It's a long, long story," Jake replied, "but I bet you'll be happy when you find out how I did it!"

"Is that thing talking back to the boy?" The Neubraman husband asked his wife. "Because I don't hear anything." His wife, eyes fixed on the monster, shook her head to confirm her husband's sanity.

"Is everyone okay?" Ani spoke to the crowd's minds, scaring all of them except the three friends.

"Yeah, we're good, we're good!" Noah yelled to him, giving a high thumbs up. "We're just about to take this train back to Orwell. And look! All these people want to join us!"

"That's wonderful." The Mothman addressed the crowd. "It is nice to meet all of you. My name is Ani."

"Ani?" Mark questioned, looking around at the others in confusion. "I thought you were the Mothman!"

"I am." Ani answered. "But before I took this form, I was known as Ani."

"Oh, okay." Mark let go. "Um, can we get a picture?"

Ali did her best to hide a chuckle.

"Maybe when we get back to Orwell, we can talk about that." Ani replied.

"Well, hey, I say let's get goin', then!" Jake said enthusiastically, turning back toward Ani. "I doubt you're ridin' with us, right? I figure you'd prefer flying."

"I'll fly." The Mothman confirmed.

"Okay." Jake replied. "Thanks for comin'. I didn't mean to drag you out here all this way. I was just really worried we were going to need your help, but we ended up figuring it all out by ourselves. But...if it's any help...at least you were here to show everyone that we weren't lying about you..."

"I always had faith in you." Ani told Jake. "And I'm happy I was of help to you, too. Now, let's get out of here and go home. We've got a lot of work to do."

Jake gave the Mothman one more hug. "See ya back in Orwell!" He said as he climbed down the ladder.

· · · · • · • · • · · ·

Meanwhile, one of the guards finally snapped out of his trance and remembered his job duties. He pulled out his comm device, not taking his eyes off the beast for one second in case it moved toward him.

"Hey, uh," the guard spoke into the machine, "there's this big, um, bird human...on the train?"

A voice responded through the device. "Bird human? David, are you feeling okay?"

"I'm, um, I'm being serious, sir." David held a dead stare at the Mothman. "There's this big black bug...bird person on top of the train."

"Well shoo it off." The voice replied hastily.

The other guard grabbed the device. "Sir, there will be NO shooing. I repeat, NO shooing at all. This thing is *huge*. I don't think a gun could take this thing down."

"What's going on?" A different voice, female, said through the device.

"I just *said*..." The guard was annoyed by their unhelpfulness. "It's a bird...bug...thing. A black...bird...bug person."

"Does it have red eyes?"

"Uh, yeah." The second guard answered. "How did you know that?"

There was no answer on the other line.

"Hello?" He asked into the device. "Is anyone coming to give us backup?"

· · • • · · • · • • · ·

During the conversation, the Neubraman family had boarded the train, along with Mark, Abigail, and her friend. They watched as the Mothman lifted off into the sky and began soaring in circles above the city.

"Mommy, was that a bug?" Daphne asked her mom as they took their seats.

"I think that was a friend of these kids." Jordan told her daughter. "That was a little scary, wasn't it?"

"Yeah..." Daphne agreed. "But he was a nice bug."

"He was, wasn't he?" Her mom confirmed. "Alright, go ahead and sit down. We're going on a train ride! And look! See the bug man out there?" Jordan pointed out the window toward the horizon. Daphne pushed her nose against the window, straining for the best view. "Isn't he flying really high?" She asked.

"Yeah! Wow!" Daphne responded, mesmerized.

· · • • · · • · • · ·

"We're ready to go!" Ali called out to the conductor at front end of the train. The conductor gave a salute to her and checked to make sure no one was left on the platform.

Noah walked on first, then Jake, and Ali took one last look around before she boarded.

"Alright, y'all. Let's go home!" Jake yelled to the group, who gave some celebratory applause as they all took their seats.

The train picked up momentum on the tracks, carrying the group toward Orwell. The entire train had an air of optimism inside. Every person on board was excited to see their families, to spend time with old friends, to feel the comfort of their hometowns, and to start this new chapter of their lives.

· · · · ● · ● · · · ·

Not thirty seconds after the group had begun traveling away from Huxley, Nimkii arrived at the train station.

"Where is he?" She asked the guards telepathically and in a hurry.

"The...bug...person?" The guard asked, dumbly.

"Yes, the bug person!" She replied with strong impatience.

"He, uh, flew up and went...that way." The man pointed.

She turned around and looked for her brother in the horizon, but she couldn't find him. She snapped back around.

"Was he with anyone?" She asked the guard's mind.

"Yeah, that girl you asked us to ready the train for...she seemed to have recruited a bunch of people to leave the city and go back to West Virginia with her. When the bug man showed up, they all got on the train, so I guess they were waitin' on him."

Nimkii pivoted back to face the direction the man pointed, searching the sky, her mind racing a million miles an hour, trying to understand what was going on. "He's trying to take people away from what I've built…" She thought, whipping back around toward the guards.

"Why didn't you alert your supervisor?" She asked angrily.

"Um…Captain Balázs, ma'am?" The guard asked in a scared voice. "He's still up in Eschaton tryin' to find those kids…"

Nimkii's fire burned hot with annoyance. "They've taken all of us for fools…" She thought. "Ani has been using these children to distract us while he steals our citizens right out from under our noses."

She looked back up at the guard. "Call your captain. Tell him to come back to Huxley immediately. I know where the kids are."

"Yes ma'am." The guard replied, picking up his comm device and placing a call to Balázs.

"As for the bug man who just left with that train," she said, "I'm going to take care of him."

· · · ● · ● · ● · · ·

Meanwhile, Ani was cruising in the sky ahead of the train, happy that the kids were safe, and was feeling extremely proud of them for what they had accomplished. There was a train car below him that was full of people ready to make a difference in the place he loved. And that, for him, was a small miracle.

· · · • · • · • · ·

Jake was gazing up at the Mothman's flight from the train window, feeling very similar sentiments about him and his friends. They had gained a new-found confidence in themselves, having succeeded in their quest, despite the differing views and relationships they held toward the place they called home. Jake released a slight grin as he watched his moth friend majestically soar above him.

· · • · • · • · ·

The train passed through the tunnel, then made its way into the curvy mountain tracks that were minutes away from the Great Bridge.

Mothman was already soaring over the bridge ahead of them, putting on quite a display for the audience below, when a lightning bolt fell out of nowhere and struck his right wing. The passengers gasped in terror as they watched the great monster fall out of the sky.

"Ani!" Jake yelled with his face glued to the glass. "Guys, Ani's been hit!" He called out to anyone not paying attention. "It's gotta be Nimkii!"

"Ah crap." Noah said, moving over to the seat behind Jake to get the same view. "This is bad."

"This is *really* bad." Jake corrected, turning back to look at Noah. "We have to help him."

"What are we supposed to do?" Ali intervened. "We're stuck in here and he's *really* far ahead of us."

They all looked at each other for a moment, trying to think of a way to help their friend – before simultaneously realizing Ani was the only one powerful enough to confront his sister. He was alone in this fight.

· · · ● · ● · ● · · ·

Ani, stunned by the impact of the lightning bolt, fell fast, and collided on the Great Bridge below, his ribs slamming into one of the railroad tracks. He rolled onto his back as Nimkii flew into view above him.

"What do you think you're doing?" She asked angrily.

"I'm trying to save our home." He said to her, wincing in pain from his scorched wing. "Why did you hit me?!"

"It's not *our* home." Nimkii fired back, ignoring his question. "You're trying to save *your* home. And yet here you are, taking people away from *my* home, acting like you're surprised that *I'm* angry."

"Me?! Ani defended. "You have been taking people away from our *actual* home for years now!"

"I haven't been doing *anything* like that!" She said bitterly. "I just built a city...it's not my fault that these people *chose* with their own *free will* to move there, because they know it's a better life for them than living in that dump you call home!"

"It's not a dump!" Ani argued, feeling the broken bones in his chest. "It just needs a little help."

"Come on, Ani..." Nimkii shook her head at him. "It's an unhealthy ancient relic of a place compared to my city, and you know it. You just won't admit it because you still can't forgive yourself for what happened to mom and dad. You have a massive savior complex when it comes to that state – like if you can stay in the muck and clean it up *just right*, that suddenly everything will go back to how it was – that it will bring our parents back, that it will bring me back, and that everything will be just as happy and paradisal as it was before we did what we did. Well guess what? *It won't*, and I just don't see how you don't get that. I've moved on, and here you are, thousands of years later, still trying to get back what you lost. Well, get over it, Ani...it's *all gone*!"

· · · · • · • · · · ·

Jake was watching the lightning god stare down at her brother, each second feeling like an eternity to him, knowing deep inside that something was going to blow up at any moment. He thought hard, trying to find a way to resolve the conflict before someone got even more hurt – or worse, killed. He ran to the storage car on the train and unloaded the bag with Kanati's head.

"Kanati, Ani and Nimkii are fighting." He said into the bag as he scrambled to open it. "Please, do something."

"Show me where they are." The godhead demanded.

Jake hurried toward the middle of the car and popped the emergency window open on the side of the train. He held Kanati's head firmly as he extended it outside of the car, trying to let the nature god see what was happening ahead of them.

"What are these things I'm seeing?" Kanati yelled over the train sounds and the wind.

"They are your kids." Jake yelled back to him. "They were deformed and exiled for what they did to you."

Kanati's eyes closed, feeling thousands of years of pain for his children. "They should not have suffered so." He spoke.

"I agree, but they're about to kill each other!" Jake called to him. "You have to help them. Please, get them to stop!"

"I can't help them." Kanati yelled over the wind as he looked ahead. "They're too far away. They have to figure this out between themselves."

"But she's going to kill him!" Jake yelled back. "Please!"

Kanati, full of hurt from seeing his family so broken and in danger, said, "Okay, let me try to think of something."

· · · ● · ● · · · ·

Back on the tracks, Ani had finally managed to stand up. There was a hole burned into his wing, and he felt every nerve frying around it.

"You don't have to prove anything to us anymore." Ani said to his sister. "We all know how much good you're capable of creating. Dad knew it. Mom knew it. And now you've hurt the last part of your family who knows it, all because you still think we're holding you back."

"But you all don't get it." Nimkii strained. "You *have* been holding me back! The people who live in Huxley are *so* happy. They don't have all the sadness and trouble that the humans have back home. I've been right this *whole time*. And now you're trying to take these people back into the same forsaken misery from which they came!"

"My goodness, you seriously don't get it!" Ani fired back. "It's great that the people in your city enjoy what you've built, but you have to realize that *different people want different things*. Some people don't want all the cool gadgets and fancy cities. Some people want to live more naturally. They want to live lives out of doors, have backyard bonfires with their families, sing karaoke at dirty dive bars. And they'll be happy doing that. And that's *fine*. That's their life! And we have to respect their choices. You have to stop seeing these people as sad, uneducated people waiting for liberation and start seeing them for what they really are – just people who find happiness in things that *you don't*. Not everyone wants to live in your world."

Nimkii became even more frustrated at his attack on her creation, one she knew was truly one of the greatest marvels on the planet, one that so many people wanted to be a part of. It hurt her pride. It hurt her ambition.

"I'm so tired of this!" She outlashed, as the flames on her head and arms grew hotter. "Your stupid nostalgia for that backwards, outdated place is the only reason it's still in the dark. The people there *are* miserable. Some just don't see it because people like you won't let them. You would prefer to keep them dumb, blind, and far away from the beautiful lives they can have with me. The second your backwards mentality dies is the second the humans can finally evolve into what they always had the potential to be."

As she said that, a storm cloud began forming over the bridge.

"Nimkii, what are you doing?" Ani asked fearfully.

"I think it's about time you stopped holding all of us back." Nimkii answered with determination in her eyes.

She brought a charge of lightning down from the cloud and whipped it at Ani, who jumped away from the attack as a large piece of the concrete bridge blasted into the air and fell around him.

Ani reacted by clapping his wings together, sending a large burst of air towards Nimkii that pushed her higher into the sky and away from the bridge.

"Are you serious?!" Ani shouted. "I'm your brother!"

"Yeah, then where have you been all these years?" She asked. "Don't act like you all-of-a-sudden care about me when it's convenient. You're just pleading for your life so you can trick me like the others – so you can hold *me* back from *all that I can be.*"

Nimkii raised her hand again to send down another bolt, but as she did, a horde of ravens began cycloning around her, obstructing her view of the bridge.

· · · • · • · · ·

"Holy cow, Kanati!" Jake yelled to the godhead, who was emitting a low hum into the mountains. "It's working!"

· · · • · • · · ·

Nimkii, annoyed by the orbiting mass of birds, shot a lightning bolt through the cyclone in an attempt to scare them off. The stray bolt that left her palm hit the caboose of the train and shook it violently. Jake was slammed against the side of the car and, out of pain, let go of Kanati's head, which plummeted into the descending mountain hillside.

"Oh, no, no, no!" He yelled, looking back up to see the horde of ravens disperse as their summoner Kanati rolled into massive ravine.

The ravens' dismissal returned Nimkii's visibility of the surrounding area, but as she looked down, she noticed that her brother, who had been standing on the bridge below, was no longer there. Just as she realized he was gone, a massive pulse of wind slammed into her from behind and shot her like a missile into the top of the bridge. Ani had managed to fly behind her during Kanati's distraction.

As Nimkii collided with the concrete on the bridge, her face slammed into the ground, shattering one of the lenses in her goggles and exposing one of her dark old eyes. Her body clipped the train track during the landing, which sent a large vertical crack running up the patinaed copper. She rolled onto her back, aching in pain, as her brother soared down to where she lied.

Nimkii remained dazed by the impact as Ani landed on the bridge and walked up to her. He knew the train would be crossing the bridge at any moment, which meant that he needed to get her out of the way before it arrived.

Having spent so much time away from his cursed sister, Ani forgot about the nature of her punishment. The thunder god reached down and grabbed his sister's suit, immediately causing a searing sound to emit from his hands as they were cooked by the piping hot metal. He panicked and let go in an attempt to stop the intense pain that was latently ramping into his hands. He clenched his fists in agony and closed his eyes, trying to bear the intense burning he felt.

Nimkii, seeing her chance to reverse the situation, grabbed on to one of Ani's broken legs with her fiery hand and dragged him up into the air, melting the outside of his leg as she pulled him into the sky and threw him forty yards above her head. Like a shot put, the goddess hurled a lightning bolt from her palm, striking her brother in his left shoulder, causing his body to twist in the air as he fell back toward Earth.

Ani flapped his one functional wing to maintain his fall but still slammed hard onto the tracks below. He laid there, miserable from the pain, hardly able to move from the multitude of injuries. Nimkii hovered high above him as she watched him lie helplessly on the bridge in the same spot she had been moments ago.

"Can't you see, brother?" She asked him. "The things that are strong and modern need to survive, and the things that are weak and outdated need to die. That means you, this state, and all those people who were dumb enough to follow you." Her one eye that had been exposed in the broken goggle was twinging with hate.

Nimkii raised her hands up and began charging herself with lightning bolts in the exact same way she had done when the kids had arrived in Huxley two days ago. As every bolt struck the goddess, a multi-colored electrical field grew larger and larger around her, surrounding her body in a bright aura of absolute power.

When the energy field was at its critical limit, she ceased the lightning strikes and took one last look at her brother below, ready at any moment to send the unstoppable beam of energy his way. Ani was struggling to stand up on the bridge beneath her. As he looked up at the sphere of energetic doom lurking above him, the redness from Ani's eyes began to fade.

Nimkii, gazing down her dying brother below, saw his now-yellow eyes and realized the Mothman had reached the end of his journey.

"How ironic it must be." She said as a white glare flashed over her eyes. "That the moth is the one who gets zapped."

She thrusted her hands toward the Great Bridge, releasing a massive beam of energy into the Mothman, obliterating him completely, and blowing the center of the bridge to pieces, sending huge concrete chunks flying hundreds of feet into the air as the train began to pass over it.

The passengers ducked at the sight of the blast as the metal supports for the bridge began to waver from the heavy weight above. The beams groaned as they bent, then quickly buckled from the pressure, taking the whole bridge down with them, and dropping the speeding train into the ravine below.

The train shot off the broken and falling rails, crashing headfirst into the hillside as it violently folded onto itself, rolled down the ravine, and plummeted into the river below. Huge chunks of block, steel, and concrete from the bridge landed on top of the locomotive and crushed it, causing massive splashes in the water below.

As the dust cloud from the fallout spread like fog over the area, Nimkii was stiff with hatred, yet her eyes were stunned by the sight of absolute death and destruction. Her blast had rendered the once bright and colorful landscape lifeless.

The deed hit Nimkii to her core. A feeling swelled up in her chest of instant regret. She felt a jolt of sorrow as the reality of her actions set in. She had done it again. In her ambition – her *stupid* ambition – she had killed the people she loved. A deep, deep pain filled her heart, and she grew weak.

Somewhere down there, in that ravine, her brother was dead. So was that nice girl she had met the day before who had loved her city. Nimkii had killed her, too. She had killed everyone on that train – including people she didn't even know. She searched internally for some way to justify her actions, hoping it would stop the rapidly-budding sadness that was growing inside of her, but she couldn't shake the retching feeling in her stomach that told her she was nothing but pure evil – that *she* was the real monster – that she *deserved* all the pain and misery that was coming her way. Nimkii's eyes began to tear up as she looked at the mangled and motionless train below, feeling the permanence of her actions seep in.

As the tears rolled out of Nimkii's exposed yellow eye and filled up the lower arch of her broken goggles, they began to turn to steam as they touched the flames that surrounded her. Nimkii lowered her head, which was pulsating with tension, feeling an incredible weight on her chest as she cried for the first time in thousands of years. All she wished for in that moment was that she could undo it all – that she could undo all of the years of hatred that she had held in and released unfairly onto those innocent people. Why couldn't she just find a way to love everybody for who they were? They didn't share her views, but that didn't make them bad people, worthy of dying this way.

As this sobering thought entered her mind, a bright white glare washed over her tear-filled eyes, blinding her for a second. She winced at the overwhelming light and put her hand up to her face to stop the glare. As the blindness lifted from her eyes, she pulled her hand away from her face and saw the Great Bridge below her, still intact, with the train just starting to pass over it.

She looked onward in complete confusion, noticing a broken and scorched Ani standing on the bridge, his eyes fading from a yellow color back to their usual red.

It was then that she realized what had happened to her – her brother had projected a vision into her mind. He had shown her everything she was about to do. But this vision wasn't a trick, she realized; it was a gift. Because instead of making the same mistake that she had made all those years ago, this time, she had a chance at redemption – to realize that attacking the things you love out of anger when they don't agree with you is not the right way to win in life – that winning in life only happens when all the people you love can have what is right for *them*, even if that specific way of life isn't right for *you*.

She felt so much regret for what she had thought she had done, but also immense relief that she had a second chance to be with her brother again and to make things right.

"Is that what you want?" Ani asked her. "To put an end to everything you think is dumb, weak, and outdated?"

"No." Nimkii said, with tears of both joy and sorrow turning to steam on her face. "No, it isn't. I'm so sorry. For everything that has happened. I'm sorry for what happened to mom and dad, and to us. I promise I was just trying to do what was best."

"I'm sorry too." Ani replied. "We're all fighting for what we think is best. But maybe if we can realize that, and work together, we can fight for what is best for *everyone*, peacefully."

"Are you sure you want to?" Nimkii asked him. "Aren't you scared of me?"

"*Of course* I want to." He replied. "You're family. Which means no matter what, we'll figure it out. No questions asked."

Nimkii smiled at her brother, but as she did, she felt an intense compression in her chest. She bent over from the overwhelming pressure.

"What's wrong?" Ani asked her.

"It's the electric field." She said in pain. "I've been holding it for too long."

The crack in her suit began to grow.

"My suit is breaking, Ani." Her voice was softer, weaker. "The lightning needs a ground."

She began to waver back and forth in lightheadedness.

Ani was panicking with worry about his sister.

"Just send it into the side of the hill." He directed.

"I can't." She paused, drifting in and out of consciousness. "It'll destroy the bridge and kill the people on the train. I don't think I can..."

Nimkii's eyes began to flutter as she struggled to keep her head up.

"Nimkii...stay awake!" Ani yelled up to her. "Nimkii!"

Nimkii's eyes closed as she succumbed to the weight of the electric field, lost consciousness, and dropped like a rock out of the sky, her body becoming a falling bomb of overwhelming electric power – headed straight for Ani, the bridge, and the oncoming train.

Ani's heart stopped. In fact, even time felt like it stopped for him as he watched his sister fall helplessly from the heavens, holding enough energy to obliterate the entire region. He looked to his right to see where the train was.

The train – the one carrying his friends and the people who were going to save his state – was now completely on top of the bridge and would be where he was standing in a matter of seconds. He looked back up at his sister, who was falling in slow motion directly above him.

Ani closed his eyes for a moment, knowing what he had to do, and found peace with his decision. He took a long, deep breath and reopened his eyes, gazing up at the beautiful sphere of energy coming straight for him.

He bent his burnt and shattered legs, feeling the solid platform beneath him, folded his tattered wings as far back as they could go, and, with one last deep and concentrative breath, mustering all the remaining strength within his body, Ani the thunder god pushed himself into the sky to intercept his sister before she reached the bridge.

"What's he doing?!" Noah yelled as all the passengers watched in terror.

The half-moth, half man lifted off at a supersonic speed, colliding with Nimkii in the air as a huge explosion of energy consumed the sky and rocked the train below. The leaves on the trees ripped off of their branches as a shockwave pulsed across the ravine.

"No! Ani!" Jake yelled as he watched the chaotic explosion grow above him. He jumped away from his seat and darted toward the caboose, bolting through the back door where the balcony was.

He grabbed tightly onto the balcony's railing and looked up as the mile-long cloud of fire and electricity came into view. He looked desperately into the eruption, hoping to see his friend – the symbol for everything he believed in – fly out of the explosion like a superhero, carrying his redeemed sister in his arms. But, as the dark and fiery cloud dissipated back into the clear blue sky, neither Ani, nor Nimkii, remained.

It was in that moment that Jake's heart dropped like a rock. He knew the truth of what had happened, but the reality of it all was just now beginning to creep up from his stomach and sit like a rock in his throat – and that reality was that Ani and Nimkii were gone – that Ani gave up his life so that Jake, his friends, and everyone on that train, could carry on a dream that he would never get to see through.

Jake's breath stilled as a weakness grew up his legs. He fell to his knees and looked at the moving ground under the tracks with his glazed-over eyes. A stun set firmly over his face as his eyes grew cold. Jake's cheeks began to twinge. He covered his face, trying to hold back tears, as Ali and Noah rushed through the balcony door.

"What happened?!" Ali asked in excitement, looking up to the sky for clues. "Did he catch her?" She looked down at Jake and saw how red his hands were from the pressure he was pushing into his face. Her confidence dropped. "Did they make it, Jake?"

Her question sent a piercing jolt into Jake's body that shattered him to his core, causing him to sob uncontrollably into his palms. He loved Ani so much and was wishing with everything in his being that he could have him back.

Ali and Noah looked at each other as they, too, understood the truth of Ani and Nimkii's fate. Ali immediately dropped down and wrapped her broken friend in her arms. Noah's eyes began to well up as he joined them, reaching an arm around Jake's head and pulling it tightly toward him for security.

"It's okay, Jake." A tear dropped from Noah's eye. "It's gonna be okay."

Jake's sadness squeezed his throat as the water poured from his eyes.

"It's okay, Jake." Noah repeated. "He did it for us."

The three friends held onto each other on the back of the train as it moved away from the Great Bridge and headed into the mountains. Soon its passengers would be arriving in Orwell, and the kids would be together with their families again.

It would not be long until the three friends and their ambitious collaborators would discover that, when it comes to creating a big change in something, inspiration is the first step, and it is often the easiest – that a long road of hard work, collaboration, and dedication sat in front of them. Ani had given his life to get them started, but now it was in their hands to see it through.

EPILOGUE

The Birth of a Principality

Thirty years after the events on the Great Bridge, Ali and Noah exited the newly refurbished factory that sat outside of the house she grew up in. Jake had been giving them a tour of the factory, showing them where *The Mothman Express* was being built.

During their time inside, the sky had been overtaken by the most magnificent hues of yellow and orange, broken up by dark red clouds that striped the sky. They all stopped in their tracks to admire it.

"Now there's something I haven't had the pleasure of seeing in a long time." Noah stated. "A real West Virginia sunset."

They all were unaware of the smile of contentment that had formed on each of their faces. Jake threw one arm around Noah's shoulder and the other around Ali's. He brought them in closer to him and said, while giving them a little pat on the back, "Come on, y'all. Let's go."

The three friends began walking through the parking lot, just letting the moment sit, occasionally looking back up at the sky, savoring it while they could. It would be dark in a matter of minutes.

When they were halfway through the parking lot on their way back to the wooded area next to Ali's old house, a slight rumble began to resonate behind them. It started at the volume of a light wind, but it built over the course of a couple seconds into a loud roar. A bright flash of light shot out from behind them as a crack of thunder rippled out from its source and began bouncing off the surrounding hills.

The event made Ali, Noah, and Jake duck out of reaction at first, but as they turned around, they noticed that no storm clouds were present in the sky. What they did see, however, as they looked above the building, was a figure standing on top of the factory.

"Excuse me!" Jake yelled to it as he and his friend began walking back toward the building. The figure was silhouetted by the setting sun, so they couldn't make out who it was. It had on a long dress and seemed to be carrying something.

"The factory is closed today." Jake called out.

As the three friends finally got close enough to the factory to block out the glaring sun, the details of the being came more into view. It wore a long, light blue dress, and was carrying a beautiful wooden staff in its right hand. Atop the staff sat a cardinal, which was obvious even from a distance by its shape and bright red color. In the figure's left hand was a sword with a golden-domed handguard. It had long, flowing hair and a crown on its head made from the flowers of a rhododendron plant.

It became clear to all of them, even though they didn't say anything out loud, that this thing standing above them was not a human. They had stood in the presence of higher powers before, and they knew they were standing in front of one again.

"Who are you?" Jake asked the being.

"My name is Aninimkii." It said.

Jake, Noah, and Ali's jaws dropped to full capacity upon hearing this.

"W...why are you here?" Noah asked. "How are you here?"

"I am here to thank you for all you have done for this state. Know that it means a lot to me, and I have been watching over you while you've done it."

"Watching over us?" Ali asked. "Like an angel?"

"Not like a personal angel." The spirit said. "I am the guiding spirit for *all* West Virginians. I am here to provide safety and guidance for any of you, wherever you may go."

"That's so cool." Noah said. "But...does that include people like me?"

"Who are 'people like you'?" It asked.

"Well, I mean, I left the state. Years ago."

"A West Virginian's heart is not shaped by its location, don't you agree?"

"Well, I guess I do, but...I don't know...I guess I've kind of felt bad ever since I moved...like I've left Ali and Jake to do all the work without me."

"And why did you leave, my friend?"

Noah looked over at his friends, then back at the spirit.

"Well, I guess I left because I wanted to get out and see what else life had for me."

"And you feel regret for wanting to explore all that life had to offer you?"

"Well, I guess...yeah...I did. I mean, I think I still do."

"Do your friends hold resentment toward you for leaving?"

"I don't know. I've always been too afraid to ask them."

Noah once again looked at Ali and Jake, who were already looking at him with worry.

"Guys?"

Ali took in a breath, indicating that she wanted to speak first.

"Noah, of course I don't feel resentment toward you." She said. "I can't tell you how happy I am that you've found peace elsewhere. That's a hard thing to find, no matter where you are. I'm sorry if I've never said that to you before."

Noah felt comforted by her answer.

"It's okay." Noah replied. "Thank you for saying it now." He turned to Jake.

"Jake?"

Jake's shoulders dropped as he looked up at the sunset once again, searching for the words he wanted to use. He took a deep breath, then looked back at Noah.

"Ah geez, man, I don't know what to say. Of *course* I want you to be here with me and Ali. I want *all* of us to be together *all* the time. I think that's obvious. But I know that there are things *beyond* what I want, and one of those things is your ability to be free and make your own choices. You deserve to live your life without expectations from me, Ali, or anybody else. The best I can do is to let you fly and hope that, every once in a while, you'll come back to see me, just like you have today."

Noah teared up as a weight he had been carrying his whole life began to fall away. He turned back to Aninimkii.

"What about you?" Noah asked. "Is there anything *you* want from me?"

"No." The spirit replied. "It is my job to be here for you, not the other way around. If you ever need me, no matter the circumstance, I will be there to help you."

Noah felt overwhelmed from the amount of unconditional love he was receiving.

"Thank you, everyone. Really." Tears began to roll down his cheeks. He tried to wipe them off. "You have no idea how much I've worried about this. And now it feels like all that worry is being washed away."

"We love you, Noah." Ali said.

"Yeah, man." Jake agreed.

Noah wiped his face once again and turned to the spirit.

"I think I've always known you were there."

"That I was where?" It asked him.

"That you were there when I was away – traveling abroad, or just feeling lonely. I don't know what it was. There's this feeling I had in my heart, like a string was tied to it and was pulling me home."

"I've felt that too." Ali jumped in. "It's something beyond homesickness. It's like my heart is yearning to go to its place of rest – to find comfort...to go home. Was that you trying to talk to us?"

"Yes, it was." Aninimkii replied. "I never want you to feel unrest while you are away, but there may be a time when you are needed back home. And, in those cases, I will call to you, and you will experience feelings just as you've described. But it's up to each of you whether or not to answer this call. Remember, you are born free, and you are always free."

"Wow." Noah let out a quick exhale in amazement. He closed his eyes and took in a peaceful breath, then looked over at his friends. "It feels really good to be free."

Jake smiled and walked over to him. "You've always been free, buddy." He wrapped Noah up in a big hug.

"Awh, you guys! Let me join!" Ali shuffled over and squeezed into the embrace, soaking in all the love they were emitting.

When they finally pulled away from each other, Noah wiped his eyes one more time, and the three of them looked back at the factory to speak to the spirit, but all they could see was the beautiful sunset above them.

None of them looked around to see where the spirit had gone. They could all feel it had departed, having accomplished the reason for its visit, and that was enough of a goodbye.

"Well, guys..." Jake started. "It's official."

"What's that?" Ali asked.

"We are *definitely* the coolest state now."

Ali and Noah began to laugh.

"Seriously!" He defended. "What other state in this country has its *own guardian spirit*?!"

"Okay, yeah, we definitely win." Ali kept chuckling.

"That's what I'm sayin'!" Jake exclaimed, looking back up to where the spirit had stood, trying to lock in the memory of it.

A silence fell amongst the group as the laughter settled, indicating the momentum of the event had passed.

"Well, time for food, then?" Noah asked the group.

"Oh, *geez*, yes." Ali answered dramatically. "I need some grub. Like, stat."

They began walking out of the parking lot once again, headed toward Ali's old house.

"Jake, know what you're getting to eat yet?" Ali asked him.

"Hmmm...I think I have an idea." He answered. "Take one guess."

"I bet it's something deep fried." Noah wagered.

"That's not a bad assumption, champ." Jake told him. "Not a bad assumption at all."

They walked into the woods, headed to the same restaurant they had eaten at a hundred times before, ready to spend the night laughing, sharing stories, and entertaining each other's wild ideas. And to them, that was perfect, because that was what life was all about.

THE END

Acknowledgements

Thank you to everyone who supported the creation of this book, in the myriad of ways possible to do so. You are all appreciated.

The Big Four

Jake Guthrie, Noah Gillispie, Carly Thaw, and Megan Chacalos

Special Thanks To

Deidra Neu, Eloise Gillispie, Steve Neu, Karen Workman, Erin LaFon, Brenden Guthrie, Ashley Haston, Michael Haston, Connor Bragg, Abigail Cunningham, Veronica Archer, Allison Nicoud, Kristian Davis, Brenda Campbell, Scott McCracken, Austin Davis, Brittany Davis, Nicholas Russo, Betty Jo Workman, and Steve Balazs

About the Author

Alec Neu is a born, raised, and proud West Virginian who is dedicated to creating fun and meaningful mythologies about his state.

His goal is to help other people in West Virginia – as well as the Greater Appalachian Region – come to terms with the existential dilemmas associated with living or being from this area, as well as to see all the potential this land has to offer.

He wants to heavily encourage support for the wonderful artists of West Virginia, as they are not only a foundational element of the community, but because they are also engaged in creating and advancing a culture that its residents can find meaning in.